TENDER TAMING

*Also by Heather Graham
in Large Print:*

Lord of the Wolves
Night, Sea and Stars
Queen of Hearts
Spirit of the Season
Surrender
Tempestuous Eden
When Next We Love

This Large Print Book carries the
Seal of Approval of N.A.V.H.

TENDER TAMING

Heather Graham

Thorndike Press • Thorndike, Maine

Copyright © 1983 by Heather Pozzessere

Published in Large Print by arrangement with Leisure Books,
a division of Dorchester Publishing Co., Inc.

Thorndike Press Large Print Famous Authors Series.

The text of this Large Print edition is unabridged.
Other aspects of the book may vary from the original edition.

Set in 16 pt. Plantin by PerfecType.

Printed in the United States on permanent paper.

Library of Congress Cataloging-in-Publication Data

Graham, Heather.
  Tender taming / Heather Graham.
    p. cm.
  ISBN 0-7862-2521-1 (lg. print : hc : alk. paper)
    1. Public relations personnel — Fiction. 2. Seminole
  Indians — Fiction. 3. Florida — Fiction. 4. Large type
  books. I. Title.
  PS3557.R198 T46 2000
  813′.54—dc21
                                          00-025196

*For the Florida Everglades,
the Miccosukee, and Debbie Craig*

CHAPTER ONE

The windshield wipers squeaked in a monotonous rhythm as Whitney Latham sat tensely hunched over the wheel, her knuckles white from the tightness of her grip, her bright green eyes wide and glued to what she could see of the road. The storm, which had been only a light patter of rain when she had left the civilization of Ft. Lauderdale behind, now thundered upon her with a ferocity as savage as the primitive swamp that flanked each side of the two-lane highway known as Alligator Alley.

A jagged streak of lightning blazed with sudden brilliance across the black sky, followed immediately by an ominous roar of thunder. Whitney emitted a startled cry and the wheel twisted violently in her hands, causing the car to jackknife on the slick pavement. "Damn!" she muttered, fighting to bring the auto back into control. She should pull off the road, but she was afraid to try. She might pull right into a canal!

"Some 'two-hour' drive!" she moaned aloud, remembering the words of the friendly waitress who had suggested the short cut rather than an extra drive of thirty miles down to Miami and the Trail. But in daytime, with a sunny sky overhead, it probably was a pleasant and short enough excursion. She had only herself to blame for rushing onto the highway with darkness — and the rain — descending. Her eagerness to manage her new job efficiently had prompted her to reach her final destination, Naples, with all possible speed, and consequently she had shunned the idea of staying in Ft. Lauderdale for the night. It had not occurred to her that the road, which cut in what the map showed as a straight line across the Everglades, could possibly offer mile after mile of absolutely *nothing*. It seemed like endless hours ago that she had passed the last signs of humanity — an Indian restaurant and a billboard that announced WILLIE'S AIRBOAT RIDES. That had been before the total blackness of the stormy night had fallen. It had been a good thirty minutes now since she'd even seen another car! But then the natives of the area were probably bright enough to stay off the

8

road in this type of weather.

"I'm going to make a marvelous public relations director!" she mocked herself lightly, aloud again to bolster her morale. "I don't seem to know a thing about the land that's going to be in question!"

She really didn't know if she was even near the land that interested her. When she had been offered the new position, she had said yes without hesitation. The job would take her away from the slush and snow of a Richmond winter — and away from Gerry. As an ex-husband, he had become as paternal and protective as a second father. She didn't need a second father. One — who had failed to realize that she was twenty-five, a college graduate and a mature, competent woman — was enough!

A smile twisted her lips despite her predicament at the thought of her father and Gerry. She would never — never, never! — tell them that she had "maturely" and "competently" driven herself into what was appearing to be the Twilight Zone. They would surely shake their heads and attempt to shackle her back to the kitchen!

Her grin faded as her gaze focused briefly on the gas gauge. The needle was bouncing below the reserve line. "Oh, God!" she groaned reproachfully, directing her comment to the divinity as if He were seated beside her in person. "Why are you doing this to me?" She could hardly see ahead of her; how would she ever find a service station if there was one to be found?

Again she berated herself for not doing a more thorough study of the area and the problems she would be called upon to solve. In theory her idea of reaching her destination and learning the particulars of the job in the city where she would be head-quartered had seemed sound. She would have a whole week to study the situation up close before her first meeting was scheduled. She knew the basics. Her firm, T and C Development, had purchased land from the federal government. The company was planning a wonderful family community, but now the land was in dispute. The Seminole Indians were claiming that prime portions of the land belonged to them. Rather than anticipate long years of court battles, T and C had decided first to attempt to deal with the Indians on their own. Hence the PR.

Whitney didn't doubt her capabilities for a minute. She loved dealing with people, and with T and C behind her, she was sure she could work out a deal beneficial to both parties. In her two years with the company she had worn down the top brass of some of the nation's most influential corporations; surely she could handle a small tribe of Indians!

Although Whitney wasn't aware of what it was that made her so perfect for her work, an outside observer could have easily told her. Of medium height and slight build, she was a willowy beauty. Her face was a classic oval, her nose pert, her chin determined, her large green eyes vivacious and sincere. The dark brunet hair that framed the alabaster skin of her features was styled in a long, feminine, feather cut that thoroughly proclaimed her a woman, while the dignity of her stature, movements and cool, quiet voice announced that she was not one to be dealt with lightly. She tackled each new problem with vital energy, intuitively looking beyond the obvious, objectively open to thoughts and ideas other than her own.

Whitney was inching along now, the rain having become a solid sheet of gray which her bright lights illuminated but failed to penetrate. The car practically came to a stop as she chewed her lip nervously and decided she would have to pull off the road and onto the embankment. Carefully she braked and hedged the wheel to the right. She breathed a sigh of relief as the auto halted without sinking into the muck. The ground of the embankment was sturdy.

Leaving the emergency blinkers on, she switched off the ignition and fumbled in her purse for a cigarette. She had been craving one for an hour but had been afraid to lift her hand from the steering wheel long enough to light it. Now she inhaled deeply, flexing her long, taut fingers. Once the rain cleared, she would be fine. She had to be close to Naples. And somewhere along the road there *had* to be a service station.

Allowing her mind to wander as she watched the pelting rain pummel the windshield, Whitney idly began to wonder about the man who would be her main opponent in the land deals. All she really had to go on was a name: Jonathan E. Stewart. He sounded like a crusty old crusader, some ranting do-gooder determined to hold sacred the cause of the Indian. Oh, well! she thought philosophically, it was her job to deal with difficult people. She hoped she would be able to convince old Jonathan E. that the proposed community would valuably aid the Seminoles both economically and socially. Jobs, schooling, and better housing would be available to all.

Crushing her cigarette into the BMW's compact ashtray, Whitney smiled gratefully as she realized that the rain was finally slow-

ing to a drizzle, flicking the key in the ignition and switching the brights back on, she
noticed a broken sign lying haphazardly on
the ground not twenty feet away. The heavy
rain must have torn it from a post. Straining
her eyes, she could just make out the bless-
edly wonderful word GAS and an arrow that
pointed into the swamp.

Frowning, Whitney scanned the dark,
cropped embankment and the fields of high
sawgrass that loomed beyond in the night.
She switched to her low beams and then
back to her high beams. Yes, just past the
sign there was a road. Creeping slowly to it,
she discerned that it was solid — just dirt
and gravel, but mercifully unflooded. And in
the distance, peeking dimly but surely,
glowed a sure sign of life — light! Almost
giddy with relief, Whitney eagerly began her
drive through the swamp.

With the rain receding, she rolled down
her window and welcomed the fresh night
air that washed through the small car. Along
with the air came the eerie sounds of the
primitive environment — the low, musical
chirping of a thousand insects, the guttural
croak of a bullfrog, the high-pitched and
mournful scream of a startled bird.

The darkness, compounded by the sawgrass that bordered her, rising several feet

higher than the car in spots, suddenly caused chills of fear to creep along her spine. She was facing danger, she realized for the first time. The longer she drove, the farther away the light seemed. She was truly in no-man's-land. Legends she had heard of the Glades came to her mind — legends of alligators, snakes and quicksand. In the sterility of a Richmond high rise, the stories had seemed things of the past — fairy tales as extinct as dinosaurs.

But she was driving into reality — a very present reality. She could well imagine being lost in this desolation, dying a slow, agonizing death of snakebite and wandering mile after dismal mile in the sweltering bog. . . .

Stop it, girl! she warned herself with a firm shake. She was in a car on a high road. Alligators did not attack BMWs. Nor did snakes climb through moving windows. Now as to quicksand. . . .

The light was standing still, increasing in brilliance. Within minutes she would reach it. Not even a half-mile farther —

But the BMW sputtered, choked and died, rolling to a standstill. Damn! Whitney's hands fruitlessly crashed onto the steering wheel, accomplishing nothing but causing tender spots that would turn to bruises. Knowing that it was her own stupidity that so thoroughly infuriated her, she still swore a spate of oaths to the betraying machinery. She had to yell at something!

Sitting perplexed, in disgusted disbelief she watched the slow tick of the second-hand dial on the dashboard clock. It was nine o'clock. The first pink streaks of dawn were still a good ten hours away.

"You deserve the mess you're in!" she told herself crossly, not relishing spending a night in the car with the frightening noises cascading around her. She didn't relish the thought of sleeping in the car, period! Having been raised in a distinguished old Virginia home by moderately wealthy parents, Whitney was admittedly accustomed to all the creature comforts.

"Competent and on my own!" she chided herself in exasperation. "Oh, for a shower and a Holiday Inn!" She extinguished the lights and curled her leather shoulder bag into her arms to form a pillow as she stretched as comfortably as possible across the front seat. "One day I'll be able to laugh about all this!" she assured herself glumly. "Now sleep! You have no choice. . . .

But as soon as she closed her eyes, visions appeared before them — visions of her running through the Everglades, lost in the woods, shrouded in darkness, deadly men-

15

ace lurking everywhere. . . .

Snapping back to a sitting position, she blinked in the darkness. The noises coming through the window were a cacophony that rose shrilly in her ears. Were birds supposed to shriek like that in the night? Chills flooded down her spine again in a mad race, numbing her. Something stung her nyloned leg and she feverishly slapped at it. A mosquito, she told herself, only a mosquito . . . but she couldn't see anything. Rolling up the window and turning on the lights simultaneously, she stared at the palm of her hand. Definitely a mosquito. A very squashed one. Breathing deeply in the small confines of the car, she tried to calm her growing unease and convince herself to turn the lights off again. If she didn't she would have a stonedead battery by morning.

Turning the lights off, she lay back on the plush interior. The car had been a present from her father, and for normal driving it was the utmost in luxury. Unfortunately, for sleeping it was too small and cramped!

Whitney couldn't keep her eyes closed. The scary, rustling sounds of beasts and foliage bore down upon her loudly despite the closed window. And now the closed window was adding another element of discomfort, it was confining her to a prison of humid heat.

Emitting a resigned whistle, Whitney sat back up. Try as she would, she couldn't sleep. Part of the problem, she was sure, was the hour. She hadn't been to bed at nine o'clock in years.

"So what do I do?" she asked herself, raising helpless hands to the faint illumination of the green-glowing dials. "Play twenty questions with myself? Why didn't I have the sense to find out what kind of road Alligator Alley was? Why didn't I study up first on the swamp and the habits of venomous reptiles . . . ?"

"Ugh!" With a shudder she groped and reached for another cigarette. Her initialed silver lighter flared high with fire, stressing the completeness of her solitude. With the smoke issuing around her, she rolled the window back down a crack. The night noises increased — the nerve-racking chirping loudest of all. Glancing at the dash clock, she was dismayed to discover it was only nine fifteen. Just a quarter of an hour had elapsed!

"Stupid! Stupid! Stupid!" she hissed. If only she had thought to fill the damn tank back in Ft. Lauderdale! But she hadn't known she wouldn't come across a station. She should have known! She should have been prepared; efficient people were always prepared.

17

"I am not a nitwit!" she assured herself. "Everyone makes a mistake in judgment at some time or another." And wasn't that what she had always fought for? The right to make her own mistakes?

"This was one hell of a mistake!" she snapped with self-reproach. Tiny beads of perspiration were forming across her nose. I'm going to melt! she silently wailed. She sat still for another moment, then rolled the window all the way down with a vicious movement. She simply couldn't endure the stifling heat.

A bump sounded on the rear of the car, and she twisted around in panic. Holding her breath, she waited. But there were no further thumps or jiggles. The blood stopped its crazy thudding through her veins slowly, and she gulped air back into her lungs. The clock read nine twenty.

"I can't do this . . . I can't do this . . . I just can't!" she whispered, her voice verging on a sob. "I just can't sit here doing nothing anymore! I'll go crazy," she muttered, the terrible feeling of claustrophobia closing in on her.

But her alternatives weren't good; they involved leaving the safety of the car. Keeping her eyes narrowed speculatively on the light in the distance, she began to rationalize.

She could walk half a mile in ten minutes. Ten tense minutes and then she would be . . . where? Somewhere, at least!

The road was high. It wasn't flooded. She had a flashlight in the glove compartment and she could keep it trained on the path. Animals were afraid of humans, weren't they? As long as she didn't bother them, she was safe.

The decision for action was making her feel better already. Stupid it might be, but it was her choice. And anyway, if she could make it to the service station, the proprietor could fill her tank tonight. Then she could be out of the dismal swamp and into a shower at a Holiday Inn.

The anticipation of a cooling shower was the deciding factor. Reaching into the glove compartment, Whitney extracted her flashlight. Her hand hesitated over a small spray can. Shrugging, she grabbed the can. Wryly admitting she had no earthly idea of what the effects of Mace might be on an alligator, she decided she might as well have the slight protection along with her anyway.

Whistling for bravado softly through her teeth, Whitney rolled the window up — in case of more rain — and climbed from the car. Training her eyes on the small pool of light from her flashlight, she started walking.

Her slick heels, attractive and smart in the city, were a painful hindrance on the path. Nor was her soft beige jersey dress conducive to a stroll through the Glades. The sawgrass and brush grew closer and closer to the path as she walked, ripping against her clothing and flesh like mystical, haunted fingers that would hold her with evil intent. Her steps became hurried; she broke into a jog.

The sturdy gravel broke off abruptly and her feet sank into mud clear to her ankles. A nervous, frantic sob escaped her as she tried to flounder from the mud, losing her shoes in the process. Pull yourself together! she silently warned, fearing that panic would soon send her racing crazily into the sawgrass.

Each sucking step she took was an exercise in agony, but the lights ahead were so close that she could almost reach out and touch them. Allowing anticipation to outweigh caution, she once again tried to hurry. A root deep within the bog caught around a slender ankle and sent her sprawling into the swamp face first. Gritting her teeth against pain and hysteria, Whitney muttered a few well chosen oaths and stumbled her way back up. Wiping the mud from her face, she was dismayed and horrified to realize she had lost both the flashlight and the Mace, but the very real fear of a venomous snake kept her from sloshing too thoroughly through the unfathomable depth of the pitch-black, oozing earth to find them. Catching sight of a foot-long piece of broken root, she held it firmly in her right hand as she doggedly crept forward again, carefully, her form almost as dark as the night, with her beige dress doused in the mud and her hair sodden and clinging to her head. "I will not panic . . . I will not panic . . . I will not panic. . . ." She repeated the words softly in a chant to quell the tremors that raged through her.

But she was panicking. Over the ceaseless noises around her, she could faintly detect a new sound.

Something was following her. Its pace increased with hers, then decreased with hers; a constant entity. Halting totally for a minute, listening with abject fear, Whitney realized that whatever it was patiently waited for her to make a move. The light ahead was close. No longer concerned with caution but giving way to the terror that gripped her, Whitney thrashed ahead recklessly, making for the ignominious security of the light.

Another root caught her foot and she slammed back down to the ground, thoroughly stunned. This time the noise behind her did not stop. A form rose above her in the darkness and she instinctively struck out with the club of broken wood, flailing feverishly.

A very human grunt of pain reached her ears and the wooden club was wrenched powerfully from her fingers. "Don't hurt me!" she pleaded in a garbled sob. "Oh, God, please don't hurt me!" It was too late to be thinking about it, but maybe her father and Gerry had been right. Maybe a woman's proper place was home, her life in the kitchen . . . at least then she would have a life! At the moment her fear was so intense that she would have bargained with the devil himself just to know that she would live. . . .

The beam of a powerful flashlight suddenly flared in her face. Blinking in the unaccustomed brilliance, Whitney choked, "Pleeease. . . ."

A grunt was her only verbal reply, but she was gently hoisted from the mud by a pair of strong, masculine arms. She was not being attacked. The arms carried her toward the light that had been her own destination.

The man holding her seemed to have no difficulty maneuvering a silent and graceful trail through the muck, nor did it seem that her weight was any more troublesome than a feather to him. In a matter of minutes she could see that the light was coming from a small wooden cabin that appeared more inviting than the Washington Hilton. Another moment and they were mounting three planked steps and the door was being firmly kicked open by a high-booted foot. Inside, the cabin was surprisingly cool and comfortable, furnished sparsely but adequately with large leather and wood couches that sat upon deerskin rugs.

Whitney was deposited upon one of the couches, and she finally had a chance to take a good look at her unknown-assailant-turned-rescuer. Her eyes traveled from the high black boots to form-fitting, worn jeans that hugged tightly muscled thighs and trim hips, then on to the powerful chest she had leaned against. It was clad in a simple, now muddied, white cotton shirt. Above the broad shoulders were a strong, corded neck and a face that left Whitney speechless with amazement.

The man was an Indian. Or was he? The best of two races seemed to be combined in a profile as proud as a hawk's — sharp, rugged and severe. The cheekbones were high, the nose long, straight and imperious with an ancient dignity. The lips were sensuously full, grim and tight.

His hair was raven black, almost blue black in the gaslight, and long — reaching to his neck. But the most startling aspect was his eyes. Brilliant as diamond studs against the handsome bronze of his face, they were a blue as bright as a summer sky and as intense as a blazing sun. They were bordered by high, well-defined brows and framed by lashes as musky and dark as the sinister night.

Totally unnerved, Whitney uttered a tactless exclamation. "You're — you're an Indian!" she stuttered. Remorse at her lack of diplomacy filled her immediately. He had dragged her from the mud and she was spilling muck all over his neat cabin. "I'm sorry," she mumbled, tripping over her words as he continued to survey her silently. "Not that you are an Indian — " Oh, God! What a thing to say! What was the matter with her? But he wasn't helping any, not saying a thing — just staring at her with what might be a quirk of sardonic amusement twitching the tight line of his lips.

"You do speak English?" Whitney snapped, irritated by his silence and the annoying feeling of inadequacy he was instilling within her. He was making her appear to be a blithering fool!

"Yes." His voice was velvety; a deep, rich baritone.

Attempting to draw on some dignity — which was difficult when she was sitting in a huddle with bare feet, torn stockings and her hair and clothing plastered to her smudged body — Whitney spoke again, haughtily, slowly, thinking out her words before she uttered them. "Forgive me if I sounded terribly rude. I thought I was following a road to a service station. I can see now that this is your private property. If I could just use a phone — "

"A phone!" The black brows rose in ridicule. "Sorry. Southern Bell hasn't installed lines yet in this block of the Glades."

Whitney's emerald gaze flared like firelight as she flushed uneasily. Without a flicker of facial movement or the slightest change in intonation, her towering host had aptly proved his complete knowledge of the English language. "Forgive me," she repeated, unable to keep the acid from her own tone. "I'm afraid I'm unfamiliar with my surroundings."

His arms were crossed negligently over his chest as he stared down at her with an austere, emotionless expression that still managed to convey to her his belief that she had just mumbled the understatement of the year. Whitney's flush heightened as his electrifying blue stare wandered briefly over her entire person from muddied head to muddied toe with ill-concealed contempt. Yet despite the anger his gaze elicited, she experienced a new type of chill — one that hinted of fire rather than ice. It was as if his eyes could really send out jolting currents of heat. Unwittingly she found herself studying his form again, remembering the comfortable security of being carried in the strong arms . . . resting her head against the rock-hard chest.

"Umm — I — " she was babbling again, bewildered by the intensity of the physical reactions he was evoking from her while merely standing above her. Why was she behaving like a schoolgirl? He was ruggedly handsome and undoubtedly attractive; that she grudgingly acknowledged. But she had met many men with blatant sex appeal. Maybe that was the difference. This man's inherent sexuality was in no way blatant or contrived. It was part of his essence, natural and almost untamed, like the elements around them.

"My name is Whitney Latham," she offered, squaring her shoulders. "I know you think me a complete fool and I do apologize. But I really could use your help — " Something flickered through his ice blue gaze as she mentioned her name and then was gone.

Something that appeared for that minuscule portion of time to be recognition and — and dislike! Why? Whitney wondered. Maybe she was imagining things. She had to be! His face gave away about as much as a statue of chiseled granite.

"There is little I can do to help you except offer you the hospitality of the cabin — such as it is," he interrupted curtly as her voice trailed away. "I don't know how you managed to get an automobile anywhere near here. I can't even get a dirt bike or jeep back to the highway now."

"Oh!" Whitney's lips formed a circle of dismay.

"My brother will be by in the morning with the airboat," he supplied more kindly, her forlorn expression having touched whatever semblance of a heart he had. The hint of a grin twitching around his eyes, he left his towering stance to move with swift grace to the left side of the cabin, which served as a makeshift kitchen with a butane stove, sink, cabinets and some sort of small icebox. Setting a battered gray coffee pot upon the stove, he added, "In the meantime I can offer you a warm drink and a shower — cold, I'm sorry to say. And a dry place to sleep for the night."

"Thank you," Whitney murmured.

The coffee began to perk immediately, as if it had been hot and ready before she interrupted him with her unexpected arrival. In a daze Whitney watched the brown liquid bubble. The night had not gone at all as planned! She should be in a comfortable hotel room right now, sipping a cool, delicious glass of wine. She should be showered and clean, pampered with her favorite soaps and fragrances, *reading* about the Everglades. Instead she was a tired, dispirited, mess! The uninvited guest of an intimidating dark stranger in the middle of the forlorn and desolate swamp. . . .

"Tell me," he said, his blue gaze unfathomably upon her as he brought her a cup of the steaming black coffee, "how did you come to be prowling around my cabin?"

"Prowling!" Whitney repeated indignantly, bristling at his insinuation. "I wasn't prowling! I was trying to get help. There is a sign out there that says gas — "

"The storm must have blown it down from somewhere."

"Nevertheless, there is a sign by your road," Whitney informed him stubbornly. "I needed gas so I followed the arrow off Alligator Alley. Then I ran out completely about half a mile back — "

"So you walked through the swamp in

your bare feet?" He shook his head slightly as if acknowledging that there was indeed a Great Spirit who must look after fools and ignorant women.

"Yes. No," Whitney retorted. "I lost my shoes in the mud — "

"Don't you know a damned thing about the Glades? Only a complete idiot would come walking out in this terrain in the middle of a stormy night!" His tone was a growl, his stare a dagger that pierced her. "You must have wanted something very badly."

Whitney gasped, stunned more by his hostility than his blatant insult. Not in a position to tell him where to shove his opinions, she carefully lowered her own tone to one of controlled anger and coldly replied, "I think we have established the fact that I acted foolishly. And I do not know much about the terrain." Gaining momentum as her irritation increased, she grated, "And yes! I did want something very badly — help! I was frightened to begin with, and you nearly scared me to death! Why were you skulking after me?" Come to think of it, she thought as she awaited his reply, he was still scaring her to death! What did she know about him? He was charismatic and compelling; he was rude and dominating. She was literally his prisoner in the frightening Glades.

"Madam," he answered slowly, sipping his own coffee, "even I do not have perfect vision in the darkness. I seldom receive social calls at my cabin on flooded nights like this. I heard you; I followed you to find out who you were and what you were up to. Then I did try to help you and all I got for my efforts was a lump on the forehead."

Whitney gnawed her lower lip pensively. There was an ugly black bruise sprouting along his temple where the blow from her makeshift club had struck. "I — I'm sorry — I didn't know what you were — you might have been an alligator or — "

The deep, mellow sound of his laughter interrupted her; his amusement was now open and more infuriating than ever. "This is incredible!" he said as he chuckled throatily. "You were going to ward off a hungry alligator with twelve inches of mangrove root?"

"Well, I started off with a can of Mace — "

"Oh, Lord!" he scoffed. "That's even better. Macing an alligator!"

Fighting her rage and discomfiture, Whitney tried to lodge a protest. "I — "

"Never mind." He sat across the room from her and turned his quizzing to another vein, still keeping his steadfast eyes locked upon her. "Where were you headed?"

"Naples — of course!" Even she knew the highway led in only one direction. "Why?"

"Just curious. It's so pathetically obvious you've never been in these parts, I thought I'd make sure you were in the right state."

That was the final straw. She had admitted her stupidity, her foolishness. She had apologized profusely for it. There was no way she was going to sit and quietly accept insults from this arrogant know-it-all! Storming to her feet with a spray of mud, she declared imperiously, "That's enough! I don't have to endure this from some alligator-wrestling Seminole — "

"Miccosukee," he interrupted with droll complacency, her outburst having amused him further rather than angered him.

"Pardon?" Startled, Whitney dropped her raving from inborn and inbred politeness.

"Miccosukee," he repeated, a handsome smile spreading across his face. "Same nation, different tribe. The US government recognized us years ago." As she stared at him, lost and still confused by his words, he added, "But I do wrestle alligators now and then. Don't all of us Glades Indians?" he asked, his bronze face guileless with pretend naiveté.

Releasing a pent-up breath, Whitney found herself laughing. He was teasing her, but then she deserved his words. She did have preconceived notions about a people of whom she was totally ignorant. "I don't know," she answered with a return smile prettily highlighting her face despite its grimy condition. "*Do* you all wrestle alligators?"

He sipped his coffee and grinned enigmatically. "Are you here on business?"

"Yes, I am."

"And what might your business be?"

Whitney decided that answering his questions could cause no harm. His frank, unwavering stare was still upon her and his queries were domineering and autocratic, but he did seem to have a sense of humor. Besides, she was in his cabin and at his mercy.

"I work for T and C Development," she said. Suddenly realizing that he was one of the Indians she would be trying to cajole to her point of view, she warmed to her subject and became professionally charming. "We have a land dispute going with the Seminole Nation," she told him truthfully. "I'm supposed to work with a Jonathan E. Stewart and come to an equitable conclusion." Almost to herself she frowned and added, "I wonder why the Seminoles didn't choose one of their own to enter the negotiations?"

Amusement was back in his glacial eyes. In fact, they were twinkling away merrily. "The council believes Stewart will represent them with their best interests at heart," he answered.

"You know about this!" Whitney exclaimed, very eager now to hear anything her host might have to say. "Do you know Stewart?"

He rose with sudden agility and took her empty mug from her hand. Walking back to the kitchen area with his silent tread, he disposed of the mugs on a butcher block and replied, "As a matter of fact, I do." Spinning on a heel, he turned to a bureau and bent with the lithe grace of a beautifully powerful cat to comb through a drawer. Watching him, Whitney couldn't help but indulge in wistful admiration. He was as tightly muscled and sleek as a magnificent animal. Probably, she mused, the long years of exercise, manual labor and life in the Glades had given him the superb tone more urban men worked for diligently in sports rooms across the country yet never achieved. What did he do for a living, she wondered. Fish? Hunt? Wrestle alligators . . . ? With his proud and noble profile, she couldn't imagine him in some innocuous occupation.

Whitney blushed a bright crimson as he turned back to her, the light of crystal in his eyes telling her clearly that he had read her thoughts and again found them amusing. "What is — uh — Jonathan E. Stewart like?" she asked, feigning indifference to his look.

He answered with a chuckle and a friendly question. "What do you imagine him to be like?" He had pulled a flannel shirt from the drawer and held it as he walked nearer to her.

"Crusty, old and hard to deal with!" Whitney returned honestly, too unnerved to lie or hedge diplomatically. "Am I close?"

"You will find him hard to deal with!" was the reply. "Here." He tossed the flannel shirt to her and Whitney quickly threw up her hands to catch it. Pointing to a curtain at the rear of the cabin, he said, "Shower is that way. You'll find everything else you might need — except hot water. I'd like to meet you devoid of mud, and then I'll try to help you a little by giving you a brief education on the Seminole Nation." Grinning contagiously, he moved to her side and offered her his hand.

Glancing nervously at it, she noted that it was firm and tanned although lighter than she would have expected, and the long, wiry fingers were oddly well manicured and neat. His touch sent another strange heat-chill through her, and she glanced at him tentatively as she came to her feet and brushed past him, her head tilted up as he ranged a good foot taller than she. His masculine scent assailed her at this close range, a pleasing scent that was low-keyed and woodsy, pleasing and titillating, a scent that fit his aura of virility to a *t*. "Thank you," she murmured uneasily, clutching the shirt to her breast and rushing past him to the curtain, completely bewildered by his effect on her and therefore nervous as a stray kitten. What was the matter with her?

The bathroom was surprisingly modern. New tiles sparkled in the shower stall, contemporary porcelain and brass formed a sink and its fixtures and an intricately carved wooden cupboard hung above the sink. Double shiny fixtures adorned the wall; apparently her host was planning on providing hot water at some future date. At least, she decided, a modicum of civilization had come to the Glades! The room offered a great deal in the way of efficiency except — except there was nothing between her and her host but the curtain. . . . Crunching her lower lip, she curiously pondered the uniquely compelling stranger as she tentatively began to doff her mucky clothing.

She was sure he wasn't going to come barging through the curtain. However rude his comments might have been, not one was in the least insinuating or suggestive. He had seemed totally unaware that she was even of the feminine gender — except to sniff disdainfully at her sex's foolishness. Any indecent thoughts had been generated in her own mind. No! Whitney protested her silent admission with horror. But yes. She — who had decided after her short-lived and stoic marriage that great and erotic passion was something only read about in books — was wondering yearningly what it would be like to have those strong arms wrapped around her with desire . . . the tight lips with their sensual play of amusement softening to caress her flesh . . . the whole of his sinewed body exposed to her appreciative view. . . .

A cold shower is just what you need! she scolded her muddy reflection in the mirror above the porcelain sink. How ridiculous! She did not — repeat, did not — like domineering men, and *he* would certainly fit such a description. Tomorrow she would get out of here and never see him again. She would forget these strange feelings that were so foreign to her . . . forget the dizzying sensations he had awakened that she, for all her sophistication and assurance, hadn't known or even believed existed. . . .

His voice, just outside the curtain, caused her to jump. She had forgotten that he could move without a sound. A soft, husky chuckle sounded. Through the curtain he knew he had startled her — he knew he had sent her blood racing.

"I wanted to let you know there's a clean towel over the rack and soap and shampoo in the cabinet behind the mirror.

"I found them; thanks," Whitney answered shakily in return.

Nothing more followed. Had he moved away again? Her wide green gaze lighted upon her own reflection. Did he know that he frightened and yet magnetized her, this half-breed with his brilliant, knowing blue eyes. That he shook her cool confidence to the core?

Appalled by her own thoughts, she scoffed but couldn't deny them. A strange longing swept through her as she peeled away her torn stockings and slip. Did he find anything appealing about her? Her skin, beneath the crust of mud, was good, soft, silky and pampered. Her figure tended to the slim side, but it was adequately curvy and her breasts were high and firm and . . . and what? Not voluptuous, she thought with a sigh.

Although confident that she was attractive and cut a pleasant appearance, she just didn't know if anyone would ever refer to her as enticing. She had entered marriage with shy eagerness, sure that she would discover the sensual pleasures of life and love. She had been sadly disappointed. To staid Gerry, the act of love was performed without fanfare, never spoken of and indulged in only in darkened rooms. Like an anachronism from the past, Gerry believed that sexual release was something needed strictly by males and that passion in a woman hinted of sheer wantonness.

Embarrassed and humiliated, ignorant and young, Whitney had buried her own feelings, the hint of desire she had learned and the fantasy yearnings she was convinced were abnormal. After their friendly divorce, she had remained cool and untouched, convinced that there was nothing to be found in the many overtures she had received and rebuffed.

But now her mind turned to her host. If she was ever to have such a man, she wouldn't know what to do with him! She would be too frightened of her own inadequacy ever to come to the point of . . . *Stop!* she silently wailed. What on earth was possessing her? She was a career woman, authoritative in her own world. The man outside was a stranger — educated and cultured, maybe, but still a stranger! Hostility had flared between them more than any other recognizable emotion. She didn't even know his name!

That thought stopped her, her hand pausing on the water fixture. Glancing at the curtain, she straightened and tentatively called, "Excuse me!"

"Yes?" the velvety baritone inquired politely.

"I just realized I'm standing in your shower and I don't even know your name," Whitney warbled apologetically.

There was silence for so long that she began to wonder if he had heard her. Just as she opened her mouth to speak again, she heard a soft rustling at the curtain and another throaty chuckle.

"My name is Eagle," he said quietly. "In the Seminole Nation I am known as White Eagle."

There was silence beyond the curtain. Whitney turned the spigot, and the refreshingly icy water cascaded over her.

CHAPTER TWO

Emerging from the shower fifteen minutes later, remarkably refreshed and respectably if awkwardly clad in the red flannel shirt, which reached her knees, Whitney discovered that White Eagle seriously intended to give her lessons. He had shed his own muddy shirt, and his broad chest gleamed a golden bronze as he sat crossed-legged at the hand-carved coffee table, his attention focused on an assortment of books and maps. Hearing her approach, he patted a spot beside him on the deerskin rug and smiled. "If you're going to meet with old Jonathan Stewart and tell him how to run a swamp and improve the lot of the Indians, you'd better go in with a little background information," he told her, his eyes sparkling with mischief. "And since you seem to like muck walks in the rain, we'd better start with the environment!"

Hiding another flush by furiously toweling her wet hair, Whitney sank down beside him, annoyed at the erratic thumping of her heart caused by the proximity of his bare flesh. Her lashes fluttering over the soft skin of her cheeks, she nonchalantly agreed. "All right, White Eagle, I may seem a fool to you, but I am eager to learn. And I really do intend to do all that I can to help the Seminoles and the Micco — Micco — "

"Miccosukees," Eagle supplied, his grin broadening. Handing her an expensive new hardcover book, he added, "This will explain the different tribes that make up the Seminole Nation. You can take that and read it at your leisure. The information is important, but it won't save your life if you do any more swamp walking."

"I can't take your book!" Whitney protested, ignoring his taunt. To an Indian living in the Glades in a one-room cabin, the cost must have been prohibitive!

White Eagle shrugged. "Return it to Stewart, then. Now — on to venomous snakes." He opened another book and pointed to the four large pictures of the creatures that spanned the pages. "These are the four fellows you have to worry about in this part of the country — the coral snake, the eastern diamondback, the pygmy rattler and the water moccasin. These guys" — he pointed to the black moccasin — "are the ones that might have gotten you tonight. They are swamp dwellers and highly aggressive. The coral snake has the most toxic venom, but its bite is tight and it can only sink its fangs into areas of flesh such as that between the fingers and toes. You won't see many of the diamondbacks if any; drainage has sent them north. The pygmy is numerous, but he's a hammock boy; he prefers the high pine lands."

A shudder rippled through Whitney as she listened to his cool dissertation. She had been a far greater fool than she had imagined! The thought of one of the vipers finding her bare feet in the muck was numbing. Swallowing, she glanced sheepishly at White Eagle, who had grown silent. His unnerving crystal gaze was speculatively upon her, and she hurriedly looked back at the book. "I can see them in the pictures," she said quickly, "but what do I do if I run into a snake outside? Ask him to hold still so that I can study his markings and compare them to the book?"

"No," Eagle said quietly, refusing to respond to her nervous sarcasm. "You watch out for any snake. Most of them will give a nasty bite if aggravated." Flopping open another book, he resumed his brisk, educational tone. "Alligator here, crocodile there. Notice the difference in the snouts. Both can be found in the Glades, alligators in the freshwater, inland regions; crocodiles in the outlying, mangrove island regions — that's coastal. Both can be nasty and aggressive, but if left alone, they tend to go their own way." Turning pages slowly, he went on to point out the Florida bear, panther and deer, mentioning a few traits of each. By the time the book snapped closed, Whitney had become deeply immersed in the pleasant drone of his voice and was sorry that her lesson had come to an end.

"More coffee?" he inquired suddenly. "Or if you like, I can make tea."

"Coffee would be fine," Whitney replied quickly, once more terribly conscious of his broad, bare chest so close beside her. The rippling gold skin was smooth and tight, completely devoid of hair. Not an inch of skin could be pinched from his form, and Whitney longed to reach out and touch it and feel the sleekness. Whoa, she told herself, suddenly dizzy and keenly aware of his clean, masculine scent. Time to move!

Stumbling in her haste, Whitney tripped over her own feet as she tried to rise from her crossed-leg position. A strong hand immediately snaked out to steady her.

"Thanks," she murmured, lowering her lashes and walking gingerly to the window. White Eagle silently rose after her and calmly began to prepare a new pot of coffee.

Leaning her forehead against the cool pane of glass, Whitney stared out into the black night. What an unusual trick of fate the evening had played upon her! Little more than an hour ago the Glades and its inhabitants had been but words and pictures in her mind. She had inadvertently stumbled into a situation that was proving more educational than any book had ever been. *That* she had to appreciate. The strange things that the remarkable Indian was doing to her unraveling composure were another matter entirely. . . .

White Eagle was watching his surprise guest, assessing her with a curiosity that would have stunned Whitney were she to know its cause. His crystal gaze softened momentarily; she looked like a beautiful, woebegone child as she stared out the window, her hair drying and fluffing around the delicate contours of her creamy face; her arms clasped tightly around a slender form that seemed incredibly petite beneath the drooping tails of his huge shirt. Then White Eagle stiffened imperceptibly; his gaze hardened again to that of a glittering gem. She was accepting his hospitality and responding with intelligence to the lessons he had attempted to give her. But she had a job to do, and that was where her interest lay. Every aspect of her — her poise, her dainty appearance, her chic though destroyed clothing — all spoke of spoiled affluence. Her attitude was condescendingly kind. A spark of anger ignited within him as he thought of her as yet another outsider determined to cause "beneficial change" while understanding nothing of the true problems.

She turned to him suddenly with a wistful smile, and a tightness gripped his throat. God, but she was lovely!

"Tell me," she said with a slight shudder, "why would anyone choose to live out here in this bleakness?"

Eagle smiled with thin lips, a motion that did not reach his eyes. He turned his back on her to pour the coffee. "The Seminoles didn't choose to live out here originally. The name itself has two meanings: 'runaway' and 'wild.'" Having poured the coffee, he sauntered over to her and continued in a biting tone. "A brief history: The Seminole and Miccosukee tribes are the descendants of the Creek Confederation — Georgia Indians. They began to migrate south in the eighteenth century, absorbing the remnants of the earlier tribes who had been mostly massacred. When Jackson became president, he determined to transplant or annihilate the Indians in Florida. The Seminole Wars began. Some of the clans signed treaties and allowed themselves to be shipped west. Others refused to be conquered. They fled further and further south, forced to the sanctuary of the swamp. They learned to live with it, adapt to it and appreciate the beauty of it. It became their land, they *never* surrendered to the United States government. And that, young lady, is why land simply cannot be stolen any longer. Warriors can no longer take the battle to the field, but the people *can* wage war in the courts with the rights of the citizens they have become!"

Whitney found that she had backed herself into the wall as his speech had grown more intense and vehement. He had actually advanced upon her with barely controlled anger, his hands tight fists around his cup. If his blue eyes and cultured voice had lulled her into believing him to be harmless, his proud, towering fury now dictated otherwise. She could well imagine his eyes flashing within the noble countenance of his carved features if he was challenged or angered.

He stepped back abruptly, aware that his

menace had caused her eyes to open with fearful alarm. "Sorry," he murmured, his voice returning to its cool, controlled baritone.

Whitney drew a deep breath. "I think I understand — "

"Do you?" The interjection was contemptuously cold.

"Well, yes, damnit!" Whitney countered. "And *I* don't want to steal anyone's land! I want to see that the Indians lead better lives — "

"Better than what?"

"Than what they lead now! I want to improve their living conditions — "

"Oh? And what are those conditions?"

"Well. . . ."

"You don't know a thing about it!" White Eagle muttered disgustedly, pacing across the room and dropping to the sofa, one barefooted, jeaned leg crossed in an L over the other. "Here we have her, folks, Miss Southern Homecoming Queen, ready to change the lot of the Indian without mussing her hair or dirtying a single polished nail!"

"How dare you judge me!" Whitney gasped, her temper frayed to a reckless breaking point. Stalking him in return, she followed him to the couch and glared down at him furiously, her eyes snapping with bright emerald lights. "*You* don't know a thing about *me*. I'm from the city, yes, and I have a great deal to learn. But who the hell are you to decide that I don't plan to investigate what I'm doing? You're sitting here in a log cabin, content and comfortable! You're not living in one of those thatched-roof things — "

"Chickee," Eagle interrupted, and Whitney saw that his anger had dissipated and that he was hiding the twitch of a smile again. "The thatched homes are called chickees."

"Whatever!" Whitney sighed with exasperation. "I don't see you living in one."

"Ah, but I have, and that's the difference," he told her gravely. "Would you mind not ranting right above me?" He pointed to her hand, which held the cup and had been gesturing with emotion. "I'd just as soon not have the contents of that thing spilled all over me."

Deflated, Whitney glanced at her cup and spun away from him, still ready to do battle despite his sudden change from anger to amusement. "I repeat — you are no one to judge me. You are obviously half white, well educated and not too immediately concerned with the hardships — "

"Stop!" he ordered, a grim smile curved

48

into the thin line of his lips. "Let's start over. Make a peace treaty." Setting his cup on the coffee table, he indicated that she should sit beside him, and when she warily complied, he twisted so that his long legs were folded beneath him and one arm stretched along the rear of the couch. Crooking it, he rested his head lightly upon the knuckles of his hand in order to give her his complete, undivided and interested attention. "Okay, now," he teased mockingly, "tell me what you would do."

Whitney returned his crystal stare unwaveringly. "I would give these people homes. I would build schools. I would — "

"You would civilize them," Eagle interjected softly.

It wasn't an angry or a mocking comment. Whitney puckered her brows with confusion. "I don't know what you mean."

Eagle raised one dark brow and shook his head slightly. "Never mind. I believe that your intentions are good, but you are lacking one basic understanding."

"And what is that?" Whitney demanded.

"It is not something that can be told," Eagle told her. "It must be learned and absorbed. It has to be lived."

"Great!" Whitney sneered. "You're telling me that I need to learn something, then you're telling me that I will never learn it!"

"I did not say that."

"Well, what do you want me to do?" she exploded, unconsciously tilting her chin to an arrogant angle. "Die and come back to life as an Indian?"

"Hardly." Eagle's bright eyes were dancing devilishly. "I want you to get to know the Seminoles and Miccosukees. So far all you've told me you know is that the Indians live in grass hovels and wrestle alligators, and that to improve their deplorable lot, you would put them into rows of whitewashed houses away from this 'bleak' swamp."

"Well?" Whitney snapped curtly. "Is it bad that I want to offer them nice homes on dry land?"

"It is bad that you patronize!" Eagle growled, his features rigid. "If you see J. E. Stewart with an attitude like that, you'll be spending the next decade in court."

"I'll handle J. E. Stewart, thank you," Whitney said acidly. "But I will find out more about the life-styles — "

"And how are you going to do that?"

"I'll visit the damn villages, of course, you idiot!" Pure exasperation had driven Whitney to the crude name-calling; that and a profound desire to wipe the arrogant cynicism from his eyes.

50

"Idiot?" Both brows raised in a high, black arch. Muscles flexed involuntarily across the expanse of his chest and down the length of his arms. Whitney shrank into the couch, regretting her snide comment and fearing that she might have incited him to violence. He stretched a hand to touch her cheek and she unwittingly emitted a small cry of fear. The tension left White Eagle's eyes and he chuckled. "I'm not going to hurt you." His thumb, rough and calloused, traced a pattern along her jawline, and Whitney quivered, not from fear but from the simple yet delicious sensation of the tender gesture.

"Idiot, huh?" he repeated with a laugh. Such a fine thing she was! Like a delicate, porcelain doll. Yet as he watched her liquid gaze upon him, tremulous but full of defiance, self-righteousness and determination, he was overcome by a sense of possessive curiosity. A strange longing really to know the woman beneath the elegant trappings gripped him painfully. At the same time he wanted to break her of the proud superiority she insinuated in so many ways.

Of course, he could easily do that with a few words. But then he would never know. . . .

A full, satanic smile broke across his face, highlighting his eyes with a handsome, rakish glow. Whitney stared at him incredulously, certain she was dealing with a madman.

"What is the matter with you?" she queried crossly. "One minute you look as if you're going to snap my head off, and the next thing I know you're finding me vastly amusing!"

"Nothing, nothing!" White Eagle assured her quickly. "I just had a tremendous idea." Gripping both her small hands within his large ones, he began to quiz her. "You don't have to see Stewart until next week, right?"

"Right, but how did you know?"

"You mentioned it earlier," Eagle said quickly. "I'm assuming you're over twenty-one and on your own, right?"

"Right — "

"No husband?"

"No, I'm divorced — "

"Good! And you seriously want to do what is best for the Indians?"

"Of course!"

"You want to understand them and their way of life?"

"Yes, I told you that — "

"Well, then, Miss Latham," he said smugly, "I am going to help you. I will take you to meet the Miccosukees as you never would purchasing souvenirs from a roadside stand. By the time you meet with Stewart, you will have a very clear and concise picture of just what the Indians do and do not need."

He was quite serious, Whitney realized, but she was more confused by him than ever. "Do you mean you're going to take me to meet your family? That — "

"Not meet them," Eagle interrupted. "Live with them, as one of them."

"*What?*" Whitney shrieked. "You want me to go live in a grass . . . a grass . . ."

"Hovel?" Eagle suggested with amusement.

"A grass *house!*" Whitney shot him a nasty glance and clicked her teeth together. "You spent half an hour telling me how foolish I was to wander into the swamp and now you want me to stay in it with the snakes and alligators and — oh, Lord! — the mosquitoes and spiders and — "

"Yes, I see that you're right," Eagle interrupted coldly. "You'd never make it. Miss Virginia might crack a nail."

"That isn't fair!" Whitney protested.

"Isn't it? I said you didn't want to dirty your pretty little hands and it seems that I'm correct."

Whitney was floundering. While indignantly feeling that she owed no explanations to this overbearing man, another part of her hated the easily read disappointment that he made no attempt to hide. Why did she feel she needed his approval; why did she so long for his respect? She had only met the man tonight!

"You're the one being pigheaded and refusing to understand now," she told him quietly, raising her chin. "I wouldn't know what I was doing — "

"I said you were right," Eagle interrupted curtly. "You are too soft. You wouldn't last a day. You'd pass out after an hour's work."

"I would not!" Whitney flared. "I do work for a living and I have for several years."

"Wow, am I impressed!" Eagle jeered lightly.

"Damnit! You think you're the only one capable — "

"I didn't say that. But I'm talking about manual labor, and I'm not sure you're even aware of the definition of the words."

"Of all the conceited audacity!" Whitney flew from the couch in a rage, her hands tight fists clenched to her sides. "I can live your Micco-whatever life-style and never pass out! I am well versed in the meaning of manual labor and most of all — Mr. Eagle — I am sure that I can handle anything that you might dish out!"

"Bravo!" His eyes were sparkling; he was laughing again.

Stunned by his mirthful acceptance of her speech, Whitney realized belatedly that she had been goaded into agreement with his ridiculous proposal. Regret over her hasty words washed quickly through her, but how could she back out now?

Holding her head high, she crossed her arms tightly over her chest. "This is a deal between us, right?" she asked in her best business voice. "We need terms. What are they?"

"Hmmmm. . . ." he said pensively, his eyes guarded as he perused her rigid stance from head to toe, a grin flickering. "I'll have to think about that. The time period will be exactly one week. If you make it, you will understand why the land problem came up. And I will help you all I can; I'll talk to Stewart for you, and I'll make sure you both come to an amicable agreement."

"That's fair," Whitney said stiffly. "Do you have that type of influence with Stewart?"

"Yes, I do."

"How do I know that?"

"Neither the Cow Creek Seminoles nor the Miccosukees are liars," he informed her coolly.

"Sorry; no insult intended," Whitney

declared, her voice as cool as his. "I'm used to dealing with contracts."

"Indians are known for keeping their word."

"So I've heard."

They stared at one another, two sparring partners, both determined to bring the other down. It was an ancient battle. Their eyes were locked in the simple war of the sexes: the keen, penetrating stare of the powerful man; the rebellious, determined glare of the beautiful woman.

It was Whitney who gave way first, but unwilling to admit any type of defeat, she nonchalantly picked up her cup and sauntered to the battered coffee pot. "We forgot one thing," she said casually. "What happens in the highly unlikely event that I lose? What will be — uh — your winning bet?"

"I don't know yet." Eagle chuckled evasively. "That's what I'll have to think about. I'll let you know by morning."

Whitney's hand was shaking as she attempted to pour more coffee. She had to be crazy! Committing herself to a week in a primitive wilderness. Would she survive on her own? She began praying fervently that White Eagle's family was kind and that they would accept her presence with charity.

A hand suddenly came over hers, steadying the pot. Whitney's skin prickled with anticipation. Eagle was standing behind her, his flesh touching the material of her shirt. "What are you afraid of?" he asked kindly.

Lowering her lashes, Whitney whispered honestly, "Snakes and things in the dark."

Pivoting her by the shoulders so that she faced him, Eagle gave her a warm, sincere smile. "I'm not sending you into the jungle to be consumed, you know. Don't you trust my ability to protect you?"

Whitney's eyes flew widely open. "You plan to be with me?"

"Certainly. Every day and night. I don't want to miss this for the world," Eagle assured her, his eyes leaving hers to follow his hand as he gently smoothed back a strand of her straying hair. "What did you think? That I was going to dump you in the Glades and leave you?"

"Well, you didn't say," Whitney hedged nervously, stuttering in an attempt to hide the rush of heat that flooded through her at his touch. Day and night! She would sleep in the woods with this man — with this compelling stranger who affected her as no one had before — for an entire week. Her throat went dry and her breathing became short and gaspy. Her heart was pounding mercilessly. Couldn't he hear it? Oh Lord! She was thrilled; she was terrified. Where was her rational thought? If she had any sense in her at all, with the first light of morning she would run away . . . as far away as she could possibly get from the uncanny power of White Eagle.

"I don't happen to have to be anywhere myself for a week," Eagle was saying amiably. With a shrug and a blink she might have missed, he added, "It's a slow season for alligator wrestling."

Smiling weakly, Whitney pulled gently from his hands and strolled back to the couch. "Will your family accept me?" she asked.

"The 'family' I'm taking you to is my grandmother. As you've so observantly noticed, I'm half white. Three quarters, if you want to get technical. But Morning Dew is full-blooded Miccosukee. She is a direct descendant of the great chief Osceola. If anyone can teach you the ways of our people, it is she."

"Oh!" Whitney said, puzzled. If White Eagle was only a quarter Indian, why was he wasting his life in the swamp? Questions about his white heritage rose in her throat, but she didn't get a chance to voice them.

White Eagle followed her and playfully pulled her from the couch. As she stared at him indignantly, he pointed to a pile of sheets and pillows neatly arranged in the corner of the cabin. "Grab yourself a blanket and I'll make up your bed. This is an ingenious non-Indian invention known as a Castro convertible."

Laughing as she sprang from the couch, Whitney obediently retrieved the bedding from the corner of the room. White Eagle lifted the bottom rung easily and the couch unfolded into a large bed. He motioned for Whitney to toss him a sheet, and between them they silently made the bed. Plumping a single pillow on the crisply clean undersheet, Eagle bowed gallantly. "Enjoy, Miss Latham. Tomorrow night you will be sleeping with the stars."

Granting him a dry smile, Whitney crawled hesitantly onto the converta-bed and pulled the top sheet primly to her chin. "Where are you going to sleep?" she asked him nervously. "I — I don't mean to kick you out of your own bed!"

"I'll be on the other couch and I'll be fine," he assured her, smiling down from what seemed an incredible height. Her dark hair was spread in a beautiful, fluffy fan across the white pillow, and the eyes that gazed tentatively at him in return were like seas of jade. An ache shot through White

Eagle with a force that almost doubled him over. It was more than simple desire for a lovely woman that pained him, but he refused to question his feelings. Stiffening to a posture as regal as that of any of his warrior ancestors, he growled a quick "Good night" and spun away in a smart turnabout. Moving deftly around the cabin to extinguish all but one of the gas lanterns, he added briskly, "I'll leave this light going so that you won't be in total blackness. Just don't panic in the night and go thrashing about and knock it over."

"I won't," Whitney promised, closing her eyes.

A few moments later she heard a faint creak as he lowered his weight onto the couch opposite her. Opening her eyes narrowly, she could see his form dimly in the pale, remaining light. The muscles of his golden back rippled even in relaxation; the trim length of his legs, still encased in the worn jeans, hung precariously off the couch. He was turned away from her, his black crop of hair resting on a pillow he had bunched beneath his head. Whitney watched him for several moments, then sighed complacently and closed her eyes. Even in the swampland of the Glades, she felt an innate security knowing that he slept just a few feet away, his easy breathing audible if she listened closely.

In her exhausted state Whitney began to dream. She was back in the muck, following a path to the light. She ran and fell, floundered to her feet, ran and fell again. The earth sucked at her, refusing to release its grip. She could see the light clearly, shining so near! But no matter how desperately she clawed for freedom, the muck dragged her down.

A noise came from behind her, and in the confused state of her dream she knew that it had to be White Eagle. But it wasn't. White Eagle stood ahead of her, framed in the glow of the light as a dark form, his arms crossed over his chest, his feet a foot apart and planted firmly to the ground.

Whitney's head turned irrevocably in an out-of-sinc slow motion. She didn't know what she would see behind her and dreaded the confrontation with paralyzing panic, yet still she turned her head, slowly, slowly, slowly. . . .

Outside in the night, a bird shrieked a high call. It coincided with the earsplitting scream that Whitney rendered as she reared up in the bed, trembling uncontrollably with terror.

"Whitney! Whitney!" Strong arms cradled

her as she fought her way from the murky depths of the dream to reality. The blurry world came into focus and she saw that White Eagle was beside her, his face unmasked for once, his eyes naked pools of tense concern.

"I — I was dreaming," she babbled, "about something hounding me. It was coming for me. Oh God! How horrible!"

"Hush, Whitney, it was only a dream." He sat holding her, swaying in a slight rocking motion until her trembling subsided to small shudders.

As her sense of fear lessened with each waking moment, Whitney began to feel faint twinges of embarrassment. Here she was, self-proclaimed rugged woman of the world, wailing like a banshee over a dream!

"I'm sorry," she mumbled, suddenly very aware of the arms that held her with soothing comfort. "I didn't mean to disturb your sleep. I don't usually do things like this — "

He was smiling gently. "It's all right. You really did have a rather hairy first introduction to the Glades. Probably a delayed reaction."

"I guess," Whitney said sheepishly.

Pushing her to arm's length, White Eagle probed her eyes intensely. "You don't have to go through with this deal of ours," he said, his expression carefully guarded again.

Whitney bristled. He was thinking her a cowardly quitter. "I most certainly do intend to go through with our deal, and more important, I intend to win."

Eagle shrugged, and Whitney could see the gleam of perfect white against the bronze of his face in the darkness as he nonchalantly grinned. "That is something only the future will tell!" He released her shoulders. "Are you okay now?"

"I — uh — yes," Whitney answered. He was rising, and a thickness was catching in her throat. She didn't want him to leave her. His touch stilled all thoughts of fear and terror. "Wait!" she said impetuously, clutching his hand. He paused and stared down at her with expectant, raised brows. "Don't go. I mean — " She knew she was blushing furiously and she tossed her head to form a fluffy veil of hair over her telltale features. "I am kicking you out of your bed. You must be horribly uncomfortable on that couch — your feet hang off it! We're going to be sharing a chickee for a week so we might as well share the comfort of a mattress for the night." Not daring to look into his eyes for fear of rejection, Whitney gazed with what she hoped was casual nonchalance at his jaw. There was an erratic tic beating in the hollow of his cheek.

"Are you still frightened?" he demanded tightly.

Miserably Whitney whispered, "Yes."

He gave a funny sigh that sounded like a groan. "Move over," he muttered irritably, "and I'll ward off the nocturnal demons. From this side of the bed, at least."

Whitney scrambled across the bed, scarcely daring to breathe. She had just asked a stranger to sleep with her. God, what was happening to her? But he didn't seem like a stranger; in the short time since they had met, she had come to feel that everything in her life before this evening had been inconsequential. She couldn't imagine anymore *not* having known him.

Hearing the rise and fall of his breathing, she wondered if he slept. He had been so kind when she screamed, tender even. But when she asked him to stay, he had been irritated, brusque. Unbidden tears suddenly formed in her eyes. Oh well, what had she expected? She had burst upon his evening and showered him with mud, then disturbed his sleep. And, however grudgingly, he had complied with her request and now lay beside her so that she might get some rest. She would lie very quietly, not even move. She would not waken him again.

But White Eagle wasn't sleeping. He lay

awake tensely, his body groaning in protest. Damn! Didn't she know what she was asking of him? His fingers ached to reach out and touch her, his nostrils were filled with her clean, fragrant scent. Every nerve in his body cried out.

Long after she had fallen back to sleep, Eagle still lay awake. He turned on his side to watch her. The rich splay of her hair was spread in wild disarray over the bedding. Her lips were curled in a small, sweet smile. Who was this lovely enchantress, he wondered whimsically, not trusting her gentle countenance. Only time would tell.

She stirred in her sleep and inched closer to him, her small frame curving perfectly against his large one as she unconsciously sought his warmth. Eagle groaned aloud softly. Sighing, he slipped an arm around her and his hand fit over her midriff just below the soft swelling of her breasts. She nuzzled comfortably in his hold, naturally, as if they had lain together hundreds of times before.

With the warmth of her body radiating through him, White Eagle finally slept. His dreams, too, were of a turbulent nature. The times were long ago, and he was able to follow his natural instincts. And when he found his beautiful witch, he simply made her his and rode away with her into the sunset.

The thought was still with him when he woke to the dawn, and he grinned at himself with wry humor. Wasn't that really what he was trying to do?

CHAPTER THREE

The bright heat of the sun streaming in through the open window brought Whitney slowly out of a deep and pleasant sleep. For several minutes she lay in the groggy, relaxed state that was between unconsciousness and full awareness; then as she recalled where she was and the events of the previous night, she opened her eyes with alarm and quickly scanned the room for White Eagle.

He was nowhere to be seen, but her overnight bag and suitcase were sitting at the foot of the bed. Sometime that morning he had made a trek to her car and procured her things.

Smiling with gratitude, Whitney leaped from the bed to burrow through her clothing. She was thankful that she was well supplied with jeans. Grabbing a pair, she delved through her more feminine blouses and chose a plain, tailored western-style shirt in a light blue denim. Serviceable certainly! She only had one pair of boots with her, and they were fashionable, soft kid leather. They would be better than nothing, she decided. They would be ruined, but they were replaceable and her feet were not!

By the time she had finished dressing and had returned the bed to its original couch state, the pleasant aroma of something cooking began to drift through the window. Giving the room a once-over glance and satisfying herself that she had left it impeccably neat, Whitney brushed her hair into a tie at the back of her neck and hurried out the cabin door.

On the top step Whitney paused and allowed her eyes to roam over the landscape. Things had changed overnight. The cabin, she realized, was built on a spit of high ground, and it was surrounded by a semblance of lawn. In the distance the sawgrass rippled in the breeze, shimmering like foam-flecked waves on an ocean. To the far left she could see an oasis of cypress trees, dripping prettily with moss. The scene, she had to admit, was beautiful.

"Whitney! Come on down."

Her attention drawn back to the present, Whitney snapped her gaze to the right edge of the "lawn." White Eagle, similarly appareled as herself in a dark blue work shirt and black jeans, was leaning over one knee as he poked at a small cooking fire. Whitney caught his brilliant blue gaze, and little butterflies began to flutter in her stomach. How could anyone be so damned, rawly attractive?

And he wasn't alone. A sandy-haired young man in a Coors beer T-Shirt and sneakers sat on the other side of the fire with a woman as stunningly attractive as White Eagle. Her eyes were the same brilliant blue, her hair the same slick raven black. It hung down to her waist in shining waves, framing a good-natured, beautifully sculpted face. For a moment Whitney felt her heart pull with the strings of jealousy. Then a silly smile of relief twitched her lips. With the re-markable resemblance, the woman could only be White Eagle's sister.

Her hands stuffed shyly into her pockets, Whitney started across the grass toward them, realizing happily that Eagle had used her first name. In fact, after having ad-dressed her as Miss Latham during their early conversations, he had also called her Whitney when he had come to comfort her after her nightmare. . . .

"Miss Whitney Latham," he was saying now as he stood with the sandy-haired man and the woman, "I'd like you to meet my sister, Katie Eagle, and her husband, Randy Harris."

As Whitney accepted their friendly handshakes and returned their welcoming smiles, she wondered uneasily why it seemed that her host had stressed the surname Eagle and glanced warningly at his sister. It must have been her imagination, she decided; no one else had appeared to notice.

"Randy is with the Bureau of Indian Affairs," White Eagle added as they all sat back down around the fire. "He's in charge of some of the cattle projects at the Big Cypress Reservation. He and Katie have volunteered to show you around up there next week."

"Thank you," Whitney acknowledged, studying the woman again as she accepted a cup of coffee from Eagle. Katie wore jeans as did her brother, but her blouse was of colorful Indian design. The handiwork was intrinsic, with row after row of bright trim.

"We're thrilled that you're really interested," Katie told her with an endearing eagerness. "When we first heard that T and C Development was willing to negotiate, we didn't believe it, in all honesty," she said apologetically. "My brother tells me that you're even willing to try life in the Glades for a week." Was Whitney imagining it, or did Katie really cast Eagle a reproachful glance?

"Thanks to your brother," Whitney said wryly, "I've learned how ignorant I am." The fiutterings in her stomach were becoming gnawing pains. They had nothing to do with White Eagle, she was ravenously hungry! "What's in the pan?" she inquired, sniffing.

"Good old Indian bacon and eggs," Eagle said with his sardonic grin. "This is going to be your last 'civilized' meal for a while. And the last one *I* will be cooking. In Miccosukee society, the women still do the cooking."

"I'm a good cook," Whitney retorted, accepting the plate he handed her. His reply was a raised brow of amusement.

"Don't let this man get to you," Randy Harris said with a laugh at their interchange. "The Seminoles were counted in with the Five Civilized Tribes back in pioneer days. They were never given to caveman tactics and barbarism!"

Katie Eagle started to say something, but her brother quickly cut her off in their native tongue. Whitney glanced at them both with confusion, then at Randy. "That's Miccosukee or 'Hitchiti,'" he told her with a chuckle, "and I guarantee you, it's not easy to learn! Then if you do learn it and meet up with the Cow Creek Seminoles, you have to

71

start all over again. They speak Muskogee, like the Creeks from Oklahoma."

Whitney smiled wanly. She had never even heard the word "Muskogee" before, nor did she know that Creeks lived in Oklahoma. "What are they talking about?" she asked him loudly, purposely interrupting the conversation that had grown animated between brother and sister. Not only did it seem rude, but she was sure they were discussing her.

"Can't tell you," Randy said with a shake of his head. "They're speeding along too fast for me."

"We disagree on the best way to introduce you to Indian life," Eagle said smoothly. "Right, Katie?"

"Right," his sister agreed with a sigh. "You will enjoy my grandmother, Whitney. She is hard-core Miccosukee."

"That's what Eagle says," Whitney mused, wondering if there was a warning in the words. Still, she felt an element of safety in spite of her niggling suspicions. At least the sandy-haired man and Eagle's friendly sister knew where she would be!

"Look!" Randy said suddenly, his voice a hush as he pointed across the lawn. "One of our peculiar beauties . . . a great white heron."

Whitney followed his pointing finger and watched as the graceful bird closed its mighty wingspan and cocked its head to the breeze. The bird delicately balanced on a single foot for a second, a proud, immobile statue against the blue gold sky, then bunched its muscles and few into the horizon. It was a beautiful sight, Whitney silently agreed.

"Randy's thing is birds," Katie said.

"Wildlife," Randy corrected, offering Whitney a wryly apologetic grin. "I can go off on tangents, so don't let me." He pulled a pack of cigarettes from his breast pocket and offered them around. Thinking with surprise that she hadn't missed smoking all night, Whitney gratefully accepted one and inhaled deeply. "Have to be real careful with these things in these parts," Randy warned, indicating his cigarette and matches.

"You arrived at the tail end of the rainy season," Eagle said as Whitney glanced with a frown at the wetness that surrounded their immediate dry circle. "For six months of the year we're lucky if get a few inches of rain. A fire in the Glades can be a terrible thing. The earth itself burns."

"I'll be careful," Whitney promised, pouring herself more coffee to accompany her cigarette.

"Maybe I'll cure you of the habit before the week is out, anyway," Eagle said, watching her expression as he leaned back on an elbow and musingly chewed on a blade of grass.

"Pardon?" Whitney looked at him suspiciously.

"You won't be smoking."

"Now wait a minute!" Whitney protested. "You keep making up new rules all the time! I didn't make any promises regarding my personal habits!"

Eagle shrugged, imperially allowing her the slight concession. "You can bring whatever supply you have with you. I don't want you running wild into the woods in the midst of a nicotine fit. You won't find much time though, I think, to laze around with a cigarette." He jumped suddenly to his feet and began collecting the dishes. "We have to get a move on. Your 'swamp week' is going to be exact. It starts at noon today and ends at noon in seven days. That is, if you make the first hour."

"Oh, I will make it," Whitney said sweetly, her eyes telling him what she thought he could do with his taunting cynicism. "I've told you that before."

"She's got the look of an eagle about her, too, my friend," Randy said with a chuckle as he scrambled up to help White Eagle thoroughly douse the fire. "Watch it; she'll beat you at your own game."

"Maybe," Eagle agreed good-naturedly, extending a hand to pull Whitney to her feet. "I put a gallon of gas into your car this morning and pulled it around back," he told her. "Go on and get anything else you're going to need for your 'personal habits.' The keys are still in the ignition where you left them. We don't have many thieves running around the neighborhood, but you might want to lock it up anyway."

"Thanks," Whitney said, dusting off the seat of her pants. "How are we going to get where we're going?"

"Jeep and airboat," Eagle said briefly, smiling. "Randy is the 'brother' I said was coming by. He and I will go hook up now. Go on — get ready."

"I'll come with you," Katie offered.

"No!" Eagle snapped at his sister, softening his command with a pleasant request. "I'll need you out here, if you don't mind."

Apparently Eagle was undisputed boss. Katie shrugged and lifted helpless hands to Whitney. "I guess I won't get a chance to know you until next week. I stay with Morning Dew a lot myself, but I have to go back to Big Cypress with Randy now."

If Katie didn't have to go back to Big Cypress, Whitney decided dryly, she was certain White Eagle would find some other place to send her. It was obvious he didn't want his sister involved in any deep discussions with her. Was he ashamed of anything, she wondered. That seemed doubtful. White Eagle was proud. He would declare what he was to the world and the devil himself could go hang.

"I'll be looking forward to next week," Whitney promised the Indian woman. Glancing across the lawn to where Eagle and Randy were about to round the corner of the cabin, Whitney saw that her host was staring crossly at his sister. "It looks like the big chief is summoning you," she told Katie in a wry drawl. "I guess we will have to talk later."

Katie chuckled, amused by the reference to her brother. "This isn't good-bye yet. We'll be dropping you off at the village. It really is remote." Waving, she scampered off to join the men.

Whitney thoughtfully climbed the steps back to the cabin, realizing she had made grave mistakes in judgment where White Eagle was concerned. Obviously he and his soft-spoken sister had been well educated, and it was equally obvious he had some type of decent income. His books were expensive, his clothing quality. Airboats and jeeps were not cheap. Closing the door quietly behind her, Whitney glanced around the single room of the cabin and determined that a little snooping was in order. Rushing to his bureau, she hastily began to rifle through it.

She was doomed to disappointment. There wasn't a single document, note or paper to be found. Absolutely nothing to tell her who White Eagle was or what he did. The only reward she received for her labors was a verification of what she already knew; White Eagle did receive a good income for something. The labels on his clothing were all well-known, respected names.

"Looking for something?"

His cool voice from the doorway startled her so that she slammed her fingers into a drawer, yelped and spun around to meet his demand with guilt written clearly across her face. "I — uh — I — "

"Yes?"

"Socks!" Whitney blurted, watching the cynical interest in his unfathomable blue gaze. Was he angry? Sometimes it was impossible to tell. "Socks," she repeated, lowering her squeaky tone to a more moderate pitch. "I only have the one pair with me and I was sure that you wouldn't mind."

"No, I don't mind at all." Sedately walking past her, he reached into a drawer and handed her a pair of neatly folded blue socks. The drawer, which Whitney had not had a chance to return to its original state, gave evidence of having been thoroughly searched. "Sorry you had such a rough time finding them," Eagle said politely.

"Yes, well, uh, thank you," Whitney stammered, backing away from him. "I'll, uh, just run out and lock up the car."

"Yes, do that," Eagle agreed pleasantly.

With an artificial smile plastered to her face, Whitney continued to back to the doorway. She backed all way to the steps, then went crashing down them with a small, startled cry of alarm.

White Eagle was leaning over her before she had a chance to gather together either her bruised body or ego. "You really do need to learn to watch where you're going," he told her with mock concern. "Can I give you a hand?"

"No, you may not!" Whitney snapped from her totally undignified sprawl. Damn him! He had watched her! He had known perfectly well that her steps were leading her to the graceless fall.

"As you wish." Shrugging, Eagle turned back into the cabin, a grin playing at the corner of his lips. Whitney winced and pushed the ground with her palms to propel her smarting flesh back to a stand. At least she hadn't really harmed anything except her pride!

"Where are your things?" the voice bellowed irately from the cabin.

"Right there!" Whitney returned exasperated. "My travel bag and the case. They're on the couch — "

White Eagle poked his head from the cabin with an incredulous expression of pure disbelief. "Whitney," he groaned, "we are not going for a week to the Waldorf-Astoria. We are going into the swamp for you to assimilate a different culture. One change of clothing will be sufficient."

"One change of clothing?" Whitney sputtered. "For a week?"

"In the most contemporary of societies," Eagle said with pointed patience, "people do *wash* clothing."

Glaring at him belligerently, Whitney limped back up the steps and furiously ripped open her suitcase. Grabbing a second pair of jeans and a shirt and a set of matching lacy panties and bra, she stuffed them into her overnight bag and shoved it into his arms. "I am bringing my toothbrush!" she declared haughtily. "I don't feel like rotting my teeth for you to prove some elusive point!"

"By all means, bring your toothbrush," Eagle said with a laugh. He flung the bag back to her and she caught it by reflex. "Sorry, no porters. You carry your own gear." With a mocking bow and quick turnabout, he was out the door.

Throwing the leather shoulder bag over her arm, Whitney followed him outside. The jeep, a new though rugged vehicle, had been pulled around in front, with the large, propellered airboat in tow. Randy was at the wheel with Katie beside him, both patiently waiting.

"I'll just be a second!" Whitney called, racing around the corner of the cabin. Her BMW had been pulled beneath a rear, partially sheltered overhang. Throwing open the driver's door, she pulled her keys from the ignition and hurriedly glanced through the car. Retrieving several packs of cigarettes from the glove compartment, she decided there was nothing else she would need — or be allowed to take!

Eagle was waiting impatiently by the rear of the jeep, his fingers drumming a rhythm on the side of the metal door panel. "Move it, Miss Virginia!" he called. "The bog is awaiting you!"

Raising a brow and tilting her nose, Whitney slowed her speed to saunter toward the jeep. Eagle's jaw was locked when she reached him, but he said nothing. Pulling her bag from her, he tossed it over the side of the jeep. Then he set the large span of his hands around her waist and hoisted her body over with the same ease before vaulting in himself. His arm stretched behind her as he said, "Better drive on, Randy, before she realizes she's forgotten her Chanel N° 5."

Whitney was shivering even as she glared at him indignantly. She could still feel the imprint of his hands upon her ribs, as if his touch had been indelibly etched into her with searing heat. She could sense his arm, so casually lying behind her back, with every nerve of her flesh.

"Eagle!" Katie turned reproachful eyes to her brother, folding an arm over the rear of her seat so that she might converse with them. "Be nice! You like Chanel N° 5!" Eagle had no response.

As the jeep pulled along the same road Whitney had stumbled upon the night before, Katie and Randy explained the terrain they would be covering. As well as the seemingly endless marshland of tall sawgrass, the Glades were also composed of high pine lands known as hammocks. The two highways that stretched across the swampland of the southern tip of the state, the Trail and Alligator Alley, had made many areas easily accessible, but there were still countless miles of land that could only be navigated by airboat or canoe. "Many independent Miccosukees live right along the Trail," Katie said, "but the Eagle clan lives deep in the woods."

Whitney leaned forward eagerly in her seat. Katie was a wonderful source of information, and their journey might end at any time. "Tell me something about your family," she begged, mindless of Eagle's stoic expression beside her. "Are your parents living?"

"My father is — " Katie began.

"Katie!" Eagle barked. "I'm sure Miss Latham isn't interested in our dubious bloodlines."

"I'm just going to tell her how they met!" Katie retorted, smiling at Whitney. "My mother and grandmother had marvelously romantic marriages! My mother's father was a businessman who came to the Glades to hunt. He became entranced by the honesty and high moral code of the Miccosukees, and finally the Eagle family grew to respect and trust him in return. Morning Dew fell head over heels in love with him and — at a time when marriage outside the tribe was unheard of — she defied her father and uncles to be with him. But my grandfather loved her very deeply, too. Instead of demanding that she desert her home, he embraced the life of the Miccosukees and gave up his own society."

"That is romantic!" Whitney chuckled. "What about your mother and father?"

Eagle muttered some sort of expletive beside her, but Whitney ignored him. Katie glanced at him with a wounded, I-know-what-I'm-doing expression and continued.

"My father was a charter pilot. He was en route to the Keys from Tampa when his plane went down in the Everglades. He was lost, delirious and barely conscious when my mother found him. She was a beautiful woman, and Dad says he fell in love as soon as he opened his eyes to find her tenderly nursing his wounds. They were married both by tribal law and in my father's church."

Whitney had a dozen more questions to ask, but White Eagle had had enough. Sitting up in the seat, he put his arm around Whitney's shoulders and forced her attention to the road. "We're making a left here to get down to the Trail," he said. "Straight ahead, you would come to North Naples."

Obviously intending that she not have a chance to open her mouth again, he rapidly began pointing out the abundance of birds and foliage surrounding the road, naming things so quickly she was sure she wouldn't remember a word. Then the jeep turned again, and within minutes they were pulling off the road. They had arrived at a small Indian village. Bright, neatly printed signs announced that visitors were welcome, and on the outskirts of the slatted pine enclosure were two large, modern gas pumps. Whitney started to smile with inner relief. They weren't going to be so terribly isolated after all!

"This isn't where we are staying." The laughing whisper in her ear sent mixed shivers of apprehension and delight tingling along the length of her spine. Eagle had an uncanny habit of reading her thoughts.

"Airboat from here," Randy said cheerfully, hopping from the jeep. "Katie could take you into the village for a minute, though — "

"She can see the village next week," Eagle said, vaulting out of the vehicle to join Randy. "You two have to get back."

"I'd like to see the village now — " Whitney began, determined to voice her opinion.

"No time," Eagle shouted from the rear, where he was busily disengaging the airboat. "Don't worry, it won't go away."

Whitney suddenly wished that White Eagle would find a quicksand pit and sink into it. He was drawing her into a trap, one she could see clearly, yet she was powerless to stop the bars from closing around her. He wasn't *forcing* her deeper into the Glades; it was if he had somehow magnetized her. He kept making up the rules, and she kept following them. What else could she do? If she demanded that they see the village now, she would be the one to appear petulant and domineering! Sound reasoning had been given her — there wasn't time.

But there was more to it than that. She just didn't know what. Either I have swamp fever or I've gone crazy, Whitney told herself with disgust. No, that wasn't true. She was going into the swamp because she sincerely cared about her job and the people it involved.

Liar! A voice spoke from her heart with an impetus she couldn't control. She was going because she had never been so fascinated by a man before in her life, and if White Eagle had challenged her to join him for a flight to Pluto, she would have found an excuse to hop right into the rocket. . . .

"Are you with us?"

85

Startled, Whitney jumped and turned to Eagle with guilty eyes, praying he hadn't read her thoughts again.

"Are you with us? We're all set. You weren't daydreaming about a luxury suite on the beach, were you?" he queried blandly.

"No . . . no. . . ." Whitney rushed away from him, scampering down the embankment to the canal where the airboat now waited, its propeller beginning to rev.

"Ever been on one of these before?" Randy asked loudly as she picked her way through the weeds and climbed to the flat bed of the airboat.

"I've never even seen one before!" Whitney admitted.

"You're going to love it!"

She did love it. The sensation of racing over the sea of grass was exhilarating. A rush of air whipped around her face and through her clothing as they passed through the canal and over miles of marshland, flushing birds into graceful flight with their noisome coming. Randy slowed the airboat, and Whitney felt that strange current of electricity as White Eagle set an arm around her waist to point out the reason for the delay — her first sight of an in-the-wild alligator.

"'Gator or crocodile?" Eagle quizzed, his

voice and breath whistling softly in her ear.

"'Gator!" she responded smugly. "Crocodiles are coastal!"

"Right." His arm remained around her as they hovered closer to the beast. Whitney shivered involuntarily. The animal was a green color that blended well with the high grass, its jaw, even as it sat motionless, raised several inches so that she could see the open, waiting mouth and its rows of razor-sharp teeth. Black beady eyes observed them in a silent, chilling stare.

The arm around Whitney tightened reassuringly. It was odd; the man teased her mercilessly, yet he intuitively knew when she was really frightened and was there to protect her.

"Next hammock!" Randy said, and in another moment they were pulling up to one of the clumps of earth, pines and cypress.

No one could live here, Whitney decided immediately. They were *nowhere!* Although the region of solid ground seemed to encompass a large enough area of space, she could see no sign of human habitation.

"Ah — home!" Eagle proclaimed, offering Whitney a hand as he jumped off the airboat with a splash. The grin was twitching at his lips at the dismay she was finding difficult to hide. "You can still chicken out, you know," he told her as they sloshed to the shore, Randy and Katie following behind.

Whitney inched her nose into the air and smiled acidly. "No, thank you."

"Don't let him harass you," Katie warned softly from behind. "You can come back with Randy and me."

"She can — and she knows it," Eagle said, his gaze upon her as sharp as blue steel. Taking her hand, he led the way through a path in the trees Whitney would have never noticed. The landscape abruptly made an incredible change as they walked, becoming an exotic subtropical paradise. Strings of wild orchids, blooming in pastel purples and pinks, splashed against the green and brown earth shades with a magical splendor. Vines and moss played upon the trees, giving the woods a mystical beauty that lurked somewhere between a woodsy glen and a jungle in deepest Africa.

The trail broke into a clearing dotted with thatched-roof chickees. A happy, musical sound greeted Whitney's ears: the warm sound of children's laughter. The clearing was indeed alive with human habitation. Eagle called something in his native language and a scurry of colorful activity immediately surrounded them, the children with their excited brown eyes, a cluster of women dressed in beautiful long garments that ranged the spectrum of a rainbow.

Whitney hovered in the background while the others were greeted with hugs and affection. Even Randy, she noticed, was welcomed like a long-lost brother. Though faltering in his speech occasionally, he valiantly attempted to keep up with the flying conversation, and his efforts were obviously appreciated.

The growlingly familiar pang of jealousy suddenly assailed Whitney. A number of the Miccosukee women were very pretty, young and as shapely as slender willows. They wore their adoration for White Eagle nakedly in gentle almond eyes.

"Whitney," he announced, and his crystal eyes came to her as if he had just explained her presence. His hand pulled her into the group, and he repeated her name. "Whitney."

She was now the center of attraction. Shy and soft-spoken, the women offered her gentle smiles. Whatever White Eagle had said about her, it had been complimentary. Eagle began to rattle off names to her, some as common as "Katie," some she wondered if she would ever manage to pronounce, much less remember. It did appear, though, that Eagle's clan intended to accept her into the fold.

"We'd better say hello to Morning Dew and get going," Randy said to Katie, "if we're going to make it back in time."

Eagle and Katie both nodded, and Eagle said something to the group before dragging Whitney along behind him across the clearing. "Where are we going now?" Whitney demanded.

"Deeper into the dome of hell!" Eagle laughed wickedly. "My grandmother prefers to live in solitude. She seeks company on her terms only."

Whitney wanted to question him further, but he dragged her along at such a pace that she found speech impossible. A number of chickens and pigs shared the clearing with its human inhabitants, and avoiding the clucking and squealing animals gave her mind thorough occupation. Gritting her teeth as they left the melée behind and entered another trail through the wilderness, Whitney felt with a heavily sinking heart that Eagle had been right in his taunts — she was too soft. She would never be able to stick out the week. In about two minutes she was going to turn, duck tail and run helter-skelter for the airboat, her last link with the known world. . . .

"This, my dear, brave Miss Latham, is it."

Whitney crashed into his back as he

halted his rapid stride abruptly. Peering around his shoulder, she saw that they had come to another clearing, one occupied by only three well-spaced chickees. One was floorless, and a large pot issuing steam sat in the middle over a crackling fire. One was far to the left with planking three feet off the ground; the last was to the right and identical, shaded by massive pines. As Whitney blinked, an old Indian woman, wrinkled like a prune from countless years of exposure to the sun and elements but as tall and straight as an iron rod, came to them on a soft and silent tread. Her eyes were as black as coal, and despite her great age it was easy to see that Eagle and Katie had inherited their lustrous hair from her. She was dressed regally in the gaudy calico of her people, and row upon row of beads adorned the entire length of her neck. Her pleasure at the sight of her grandchildren was obvious and yet subdued; she accepted them like a queen receiving homage. Once again Whitney hovered in the background, lost while they conversed in the Miccosukee language. The old woman's eyes were upon her with unabashed speculation, and Whitney's ears pricked like a dog's when she began to hear her own name and that of Jonathan Stewart mentioned.

She was surprised and dismayed when

Morning Dew frowned, angered over what-ever was being said. It was she who clutched Whitney and pulled her into the group, her gnarled hands amazingly strong and her words vehement although still soft and con-trolled. Eagle said something impatiently, then as if remembering whom he addressed, he quieted his own tone and went into a lengthy explanation. Whitney caught Randy Harris's eye and imploringly demanded, "What is going on?"

Suddenly they all went silent.

"Eagle will tell you," Katie said hastily, kissing her grandmother's cheek and grab-bing Randy's hand. "We've got to go. Are you sure you'll be okay?"

Eagle was staring at her with his bright blue eyes full of mockery and challenge. "Well?"

"I — I — yes, but what — "

"See you next week, then," Katie inter-rupted, impulsively kissing her cheek, too. "Don't worry — Gram isn't mad at you. 'Bye!"

"Good luck!" Randy called.

They started back through the path in a sprint, and Whitney was left to helplessly watch them go. Eagle came behind her and his steel-sinewed arms encircled her waist.

"Would you run?" he whispered in a

husky taunt. "If so, run now. In another minute you will irrefutably be my woman for the coming week. You have entered the devil's den, and the devil is about to demand his due."

Gut panic gripped Whitney like a wall of ice. It was more than a teasing threat that Eagle had issued. There was an underlying tension in his voice that hinted of a deep fury, as if he was extracting vengeance.

For what, she wondered.

Then, as she snapped around in his arms to make a fear-inspired, acidic retort, she knew.

She was going to pay for her impulsive words when they met — for calling him an Indian with shocked amazement, for haughtily demanding if he could speak English.

Worst of all, she was going to pay because he had read what she felt in her heart — that she was superior to him. And now there was nothing left to do except bluff her way through it. If his arms were steel, her will would be concrete. She would prove her mettle and take great pleasure in forcing White Eagle to realize he was not dealing with a hothouse Southern belle!

"Devil's den?" She smiled sweetly with mock innocence. "This is a paradise. I'm going to love it!"

"Hmmm . . . I hope so," Eagle replied, tapping her chin lightly with a playful gesture. The threat was still in his eyes as he stared down at her, yet it was tempered now with a mixture of other emotions, all of which were veiled. What were those emotions, Whitney wondered. A dawning of respect along with something else?

A shiver coursed through her. In the heart of her femininity she had finally read the blatant message of coolly controlled desire. White Eagle had been touched by the same inexplicable, electric attraction as she. He knew her fascination; he knew her fear and doubt.

And he played a waiting game, on his own territory, where he was sure that he would win.

Knowing the answer before she voiced the question, Whitney could not hide the waver in her tone as she demanded, "You never did tell me what you expect to get out of this bet."

"That's rather obvious, isn't it?" he drawled, and the current between them was almost visible in the air. "You."

CHAPTER FOUR

Whitney sat hunched upon her rock, her arms wrapped tiredly around her knees, a single eye resting sorrowfully upon the hand that cradled her cheek. She had never known it was possible to achieve so many calluses in one day, and her nails — usually perfectly manicured and sporting the latest in fashion colors — were broken, chipped and split. She shifted slightly and soreness riddled her back. Groaning, she awkwardly tried to massage the pain.

It wasn't Eagle but Morning Dew who had proved to be her taskmaster. In one afternoon Whitney had learned that the life of an Indian woman was still rugged indeed. So far she had been called upon to wash clothes by hand, tend the garden of late summer vegetables, feed an assortment of domesticated animals, sew until her fingers could no longer hold a needle and pound upon a strange root until it became a powdery substance that would be used as flour.

Not that Morning Dew hadn't been kind. She had clucked in perfect English like a mother hen over Whitney and taken her under a competent wing. Immediately after Eagle had stated his terms, he had spun from her as if the interchange had never existed, spoken to his grandmother, then informed Whitney that he would see her later. When she had asked where he was going, he raised and wiggled a teasing brow. "Off to play Indian brave, of course."

Sunset was coming to the Everglades. As Whitney watched, the sky began to take on a myriad crimson and golden hues. The colors rippled and danced upon the calm, glassy sheet of the lake she sat before, creating a dazzling display. Numerous long-legged birds, trusting in her stillness, stood sentinel along the shore, forming silhouettes against the brilliant pink horizon. She realized her earlier words of bravado had not been a lie — visions of pure paradise lurked within the desolate hammocks of the deep woods.

"Ooohhh. . . ." she moaned again, trying to shift in order to ease the throbbing of newly discovered muscles.

"Rough day, huh?"

Whitney spun with a belligerent stare to see that Eagle was standing two feet behind her. Damn him! she muttered inwardly with irritation. His ability to come upon her totally undetected was most annoying.

"Not at all," she retorted nastily. "The washer didn't clog up once and I didn't have a bit of trouble at the grocery store."

Laughing, Eagle took a step and eradicated the distance between them. Before Whitney could protest, he had pushed her shoulders back and begun massaging her neck with strong fingers that brought a mixture of new torment and sweet, easing relief. Giving in to the overwhelming urge to relish the comfort brought by his powerful hands, Whitney sighed and allowed her head to rest again upon her hands.

"Where have you been all day?" she demanded impertinently, determined that he not know how grateful she was for his soothing ministrations.

"Oh, you know . . . hunting, fishing, warring with the cavalry," he replied airily.

"Very amusing," Whitney snapped. His thumb worked into her collarbone and an unexpected surge of excitement spread through her bloodstream like hot mercury. She jerked with confusion, wondering if he had felt her reaction to his touch. "You don't have to rip me apart!" she muttered hastily. "I'm quite sore enough as it is!"

Ignoring her viperish tongue, Eagle pulled her back into position. "Sit still. If I don't work out the kinks for you, you'll be in agony tomorrow. And I don't want you slacking off around the chickee!"

Whitney clamped her teeth together and stared out over the lake. He was right and she knew it. She would awake as stiff as a poker in the morning if she didn't allow him to work the knots out of her sore muscles.

But she had to maintain her guard with this man. For the first time in her life she was at a loss emotionally and physically. She was attracted to him like a moth to flame, yet unlike a moth, she had the sense to see the fire. He was an enigma to her, and yet his motives seemed as crystal clear as his eyes. He dared her, he mocked her. He had brought her into a world where he didn't need to lift a finger to inflict punishment. And he wanted her.

The why of it all troubled Whitney. Intuition told her that a man like Eagle would have strong passions and be proficient in the realm of sensual delights. She knew beyond a doubt that he would attract any number of the feminine sex — and that countless women would be more than happy to appease his appetites.

So why her? Why go through this elabo-rate charade to win what he could obviously have for the taking? Especially when he must realize the effect his mere proximity had on her. There were moments of electricity be-tween them that were so intense Whitney would gladly come to him with eager sub-mission, except. . . .

That he was an Indian? An alien to her world? He frightened her as she had never been frightened before. . . .

And yet that wasn't it, either. If she was really frightened of something, it wasn't White Eagle. She had come to realize that he lived by a code of ethics that might put any city-bred man to shame.

True admission of her real fears hovered in her consciousness, but they were too deep to surface. Too painful. They had nothing to do with morality. In her heart she knew that anything between them would be right be-cause such a feeling could come only once in a lifetime. . . .

"Isn't it?"

Whitney blinked. She had grown drowsy and content while he worked his magic upon her body, and now she hadn't heard a word he had said.

Yawning, she perked her head back up.

"Sorry — isn't what?"

"The lake beautiful — and very inviting."

"Yes, yes it is."

His hands left her shoulders, and she felt a sense of loss. "Join me?" The blue of his eyes was very bright against the bronze of his face in the twilight as he casually began opening the buttons on his shirt.

"Join you?" Whitney echoed blankly.

"For a swim. The water here is always cool and pleasant. A swim makes you feel a hell of a lot better in this climate — much less like a salt lick for cattle."

His shirt was gone, cast over a nearby bush. "Scoot over," he commanded, sliding down beside her on the rock to remove his boots. The heat of his body absorbed her as he nonchalantly pulled at the high zippers to free his feet and roll his socks. Like an unabashed child at a swimming hole, he stood again and Whitney heard the quick slide of his jeans zipper.

"I don't have a suit," Whitney whispered, hastily averting her eyes to look at the water before her.

"Neither do I."

A whoosh sounded through the air and she knew that his jeans and briefs had joined the shirt on the bush. He was a streak of perfect bronze as he whipped past her into the lake with a clear-cut, graceful dive.

"Come on!" There was deviltry to his invitation.

"I — I — "

"I'm not going to attack you!" Eagle called cynically, rising with the cool water dripping from his form. The lake covered him to his waist and he stood facing her regally, his hands planted firmly on his hips. His hair was slicked back by the water, defining the rugged lines of his profile as he grinned.

Whitney fought the blush that was rising to her cheeks. He was laughing at her, mocking her fear.

"What about snakes?" she countered.

"This pool is clear," he assured her. "And I'll be with you."

Whitney hesitated slightly, an eyetooth gnawing at her lip. He definitely wasn't going to attack her — he was almost contemptuous of her — which wasn't particularly flattering! The water did look inviting, and the humid temperature of the Glades *had* left her feeling like a large salt deposit. She rose slowly and dully set to work on the snaps of her tailored blouse.

If she had expected him to turn away, she was in for a surprise. He watched her every movement intently, his hands still upon his hips, his magnetizing eyes still bright with amusement — and appreciation. Whitney managed to doff her shirt, jeans and boots with nonchalance; then she froze, inhibited despite his words of assurance.

Eagle laughed again as she stood on the shore in panties and bra, confused. Yet he wasn't laughing at her, she realized, but rather with a sympathetic understanding.

"Okay!" she yelled at him, assessing the communication for what it was. "You could make this a little easier for me by taking a big jump into the lake — deep!"

He shook his head sternly. "You are beautiful, Whitney. Very fine, very delicate. Don't hide from me."

Unnerved by his bluntness, Whitney felt the blush of her cheeks spread through her body. "Does that mean I have no right to be modest?" she mumbled sarcastically, lowering her head as she fumbled for the hook of her bra.

His answer was soft. "No, Whitney. But we are hardly strangers. You know that as well as I."

Unable to meet his eyes, Whitney dropped the white lacy bra to her feet and slipped from the brief bikini pants with an inborn sensuality that would have stunned her were she aware of it. There was a sharp whistle of air on the wind, but as she wasn't watching White Eagle, she didn't know that the sound had been that of his indrawn breath.

Eagle was thinking that her suggestion that he jump more deeply into the lake might be just what he needed. He had just calmly informed her that he would not touch her, but he had never felt a more potent rush of pure desire in his life. His natural comment that she was beautiful had been a tremendous understatement — she surpassed any terminology in any language. "Gorgeous" would not sufficiently describe her. Although slender and petite, she was built with subtle voluptuousness; her breasts were not heavy but high and firm, rosy-tipped, her hips trim and yet ever so pleasantly rounded. Her legs were long and shapely, graceful like those of a gazelle. She had been married for a year, he knew — he knew a great deal about her, in fact. Yet about her there was an air of innocence. Of trust. She could be feisty, proud, arrogant and haughty. Still . . . that beguiling essence remained with her. . . .

A flash of heat that ripped through him in spasms assailed Eagle with crude violence as she sprinted into the water. Impatiently he cursed at himself, raised his arms high and plunged into the depths of the lake. With powerful strokes he whipped through the water, not surfacing until he had vigorously brought his telling body back into a semblance of control.

The water was delicious, Whitney decided instantly, relishing in its wonderfully cool feeling upon her skin. Not the swimmer that Eagle was, she contented herself with splashing around near the shore. Rising after a moment to shield her eyes against the setting sun and scan the lake for White Eagle, she frowned. "Where the hell is he, anyway?" she muttered.

Beneath her, she discovered an immediate reply as her ankle was deftly wrenched and she tumbled full length into the lake. Sputtering and choking, she kicked her way back up and sought her adversary. He was about a foot away, chuckling. Without bothering to think, she threw herself at him, determined to douse his smug face beneath the surface.

But he had anticipated her impulsive response and he caught her, his hands strong against her midriff. He held her inches away, with the peaks of her nipples brushing the smoothness of his chest, gloating. For a split second he kept her there, and their eyes met in elemental challenge. Then she was once more doused.

Fuming beneath the surface, Whitney swam as far as her lungs would carry her. When she finally broke above the water, he was still watching her, still smiling smugly, still gloating. To him there was no contest.

"Never attack a stronger enemy!" he said with a laugh, verifying her thoughts. "Use strategy!" Then he was swimming away again, the certain victor.

Strategy, Whitney silently repeated. She would use strategy all right, strategy and patience. It would be a dangerous battle, but she couldn't resist. He had the galling capacity to make her forget logic and reason and respond with pure warlike tactics. But she did intend to win — even the little battles, the skirmishes.

When he surfaced again and looked for her, she laughed enchantingly.

"You're right!" she called gaily. "I never will get you under!" Smiling with coquettish invitation, she began an easy sidestroke, emphasizing the languorousness of her movements.

As she had planned, he swam toward her. As she hadn't planned, his nearness threw her completely. The water itself heated between them, like a whirling hot tub. She was painfully aware of his powerful sleekness, swallowing to resist the temptation to run her hands along the glistening limbs that moved beside her.

Strategy! she reminded herself coolly, inching back to a depth where she could stand. A little thrill shot its way exultantly to her mind as she remembered his tone when he had told her she was beautiful. In her little game of retaliation, she didn't intend to make him lose control, she simply wanted to draw on a few of his instincts. Just draw him a few little inches into her lair. . . .

Purposely she slowly brushed against him as they both found their footing. It was a dangerous game. The contact of his bare flesh was exhilarating; her own instincts screamed that she cling to it.

But she faced him instead, her smile a little coy, a little captivating. Surely he wouldn't refuse an overt gesture . . . yet she couldn't let him become in the least suspicious.

Whitney stretched a long finger to touch his raven hair, as if unwittingly fascinated. His response was gentle as he captured her hand and drew her irrevocably to him. Feigning hesitant submission, Whitney inched along his frame, gasping involuntarily with a shock that had nothing to do with the game. It was already going too well. Proof that she could elicit his desire touched along the tender flesh of her lower abdomen as her legs entangled with his.

Now! Whitney told herself as she met his tense stare. Now, while she could still break his unprepared grip, before his lips fell to claim hers.

With all her strength she plunged beneath the surface, and with unimaginable speed she clasped his ankle with both hands and jerked. It was working! His foot rose and his knee bent. . . .

But he didn't fall and crash into the lake. The bent leg tensed and she was disbelievingly being dragged back. Stupidly realizing her mistake, Whitney released his ankle and started a mad dash away.

Too late. His hand sank into her hair, the fingers curled and she was pulled back, his grip not painful but forceful.

Her eyes were clouded with fear when they met his cold ones. "Dirty play, wasn't that?" he inquired tautly.

"All's fair in love and war, isn't it?" Whitney demanded flippantly. His features were tense and his jaw was crookedly locked.

"Those are the rules," Eagle agreed, the glint of his eyes a glacial blue. "As long as they apply to both parties."

A shudder of fear gripped her, but he gave no notice. The hand that laced her hair tilted her head back, and his mouth slowly and surely came over hers. Whitney's lips were parted with amazement, aiding and abetting his assault, which certainly couldn't be called unprovoked. She had gambled and lost. But how far would he carry his retaliation? How far did she want him to carry it? She had stiffened, ready to fight him no matter how feeble her efforts. But her fight lasted less than ten seconds. His kiss, a strange combination of harsh demand and persuasive tenderness, was drugging her, numbing her to acquiescent submission. His foot wedged around hers, holding her his prey, while his tongue deeply plundered the recesses of her mouth, seeking hers, hypnotizing it into a return play.

Immersed in the warm, assured command of his mouth, she thrust deeply herself, tasting and seeking, running the tip of her tongue in light discovery of his pearl white teeth. His mouth left hers to follow a slow, moist suctioning trail across the softness of her cheek to her earlobe, down the length of her neck, to the shadowed hollow of her breasts. His sleek length along hers held no secrets, and she found she was no longer pushing against his broad chest but burrowing into it, striving to be submissively accessible to the wonder of his driving touch.

His hands were on the small of her back, pressing her closer and closer. They lowered to cradle her buttocks and lift her slightly, arch her hips to his so that she could feel the full force of the virile masculinity she had tauntingly elicited against her body. A sigh escaped her, and her lips fell to his shoulder, where her teeth grazed gently as tremors scurried from her head to her toes, flashing convulsively with dizzying heat. She was freezing with fear but burning with anticipation. One of his hands moved in seductive exploration, rounding the contour it held, gently splaying her thigh in search of further secrets.

Torn by irresistible sensation, Whitney realized she was getting so much more than she had bargained for, so much more than she had known existed . . . God! She longed for it to go on, to savor the feel of him, to taste, touch and explore. She wanted the trembling, aching torment to find its way to ultimate culmination. . . .

But she was afraid. So very afraid.

His mouth moved to the high peak of her breast, and his teeth raked it just slightly. The searing sensation was so great that she totally lost her breath; and as her flesh rippled with the jolt, a fear of the crippling delight that rendered her helpless despite her desire suddenly bubbled to the surface.

Her sigh became a plea. . . .

Eagle released her so abruptly that she spattered back into the water, barely keeping her face above the surface. His face was a cold mask; his eyes were glittering orbs. "Go, rabbit," he said icily, "run. I told you I wouldn't force you. If and when you're feeling like a woman, you can come to me." He turned, leaving her wide-eyed and quivering in the water, her mouth bruised, her ego in a peculiar state between relief and humiliation.

Eagle was cursing beneath his breath as he cut through the water for the shore with strong strides. The little bitch! She had known damn well what she was doing. By every right he should have taken her there, by the shore. She had responded to him; her body had melded to his in perfect unison, her sensuality had risen instinctively to meet his. The hidden passion he had tasted hinted of a coming together even he couldn't imagine. . . . But here he was instead, rushing out of the water because he had sensed her fear. A sucker! he told himself disgustedly. A real sap. She probably played her little games a million times, and that feigned innocence saved her. . . .

Pulling his jeans over his legs, he tucked his shirt in and impatiently jerked up his zipper. Glancing out of the corner of his eye, he felt his temper begin to subside. She didn't know that he watched her, and her face and eyes were unguarded. There was none of the usual arrogance apparent. At the moment she looked like a wounded doe, lost, bewildered and delicately stunning. Her arms were clasped protectively around her chest, and her hair, soaking wet, curled long past her waist, covering her modestly like a modern-day Godiva. There was a secret to her, Eagle decided, and he intended to unravel that secret. He wanted her to come to him with complete trust. He had the strange intuition that once would never be enough. If he drank her sweet nectar he would thirst again, and again and again. . . .

He walked to her then and set his hands on her shoulders, groaning inwardly as she flinched at his touch and clutched her clothing tightly to her breast. Tilting her chin to force her eyes to his, he smiled with warmth. "Don't get all cold and withdrawn on me again, huh? You are exquisite, and I don't think you'd be tremendously happy if I didn't think so and tell you!" Not waiting for a reply, he became very businesslike and brusquely began helping her back into her bra, managing the lace-frothed hook with competence.

Whitney stood compliantly still, then

ducked quickly into her underwear and jeans. He began speaking again as she snapped her shirt together.

"You are about to taste the fruits of our combined day's labor," he said blandly. "I'm sure my grandmother is waiting for us at the *sofki* pot; we usually eat our evening meals as stews. Some of the vegetables you tended will be in it, and the venison we bagged today. I hope you like it. We also eat tropical fruit at supper — mangoes, papayas, guavas. And bread from the *koonti* root you pounded." His arm came casually around her shoulder as he led her through the pine trail that would bring them back to Morning Dew's three chickees. How could he change so quickly, Whitney wondered with amazement. He had gone from passion to anger to ambivalence in the wink of an eye, while she was still a barely controlled jumble of boiling blood and frazzled nerves . . . no, she told herself solidly, not *barely* controlled. Controlled. She *would* manage to be as nonchalant as he.

"I'm starving," she answered him idly. "I have a feeling I'm going to love that stew — no matter what's in it."

"Even alligator?" he teased.

Whitney eyed him suspiciously. "Do you really eat alligator?"

"Yes, sometimes, but not tonight. We respect the season. They are an endangered species. If you're game, I'll see that you get to try it sometime. If smoked correctly, it's delicious."

"Fine." Whitney shrugged, musing over his words. What did "sometime" mean? In a week's time she would be in Naples, back in the world of business. Her days would be full with meetings, schedules and plans. Eagle would be back in his cabin. . . .

Or would he? She didn't know where he actually lived. He adapted to his habitation easily. Was his real home another chickee in another village?

It didn't matter. At the end of the week she would accept his help with Stewart as her due. Then this tumultuous span of days in her life would fade to the background and things would return to normal.

No. Things would never return to normal again. Whatever this man was, she was never going to be able to forget him.

Little pricks of unbidden excitement started finding their way back into her system. A wave of hot panic washed over her in a black wall that momentarily blanked her vision. *What if she lost?* What if she found she couldn't stand up to the rigors after a few days of grueling labor? Was she really to be his winning stake? She was walking normally beside him, but she felt as if her feet did not quite touch the ground, as if helium held her afloat. Would he really demand payment?

God! The groan reverberated within her own mind. She didn't know what she wanted herself. There had been seconds in the water when she had wanted him to forget his words and promises — moments when she had wished that he would take her and let her discover what it could be like . . . force her into knowing if the ecstasy she had felt hints of could really exist. . . .

She glanced at him to find him surreptitiously watching her with his keen, probing stare. Flushing, she searched her mind for a topic of casual conversation. There were always a million things she wanted to ask him when he was walking away from her!

"What was your grandmother angry about this morning?" she asked hastily.

Eagle chuckled pleasantly in his low baritone. Watching the amusement spread into his features, Whitney was again struck by the appeal his face had for her. It wasn't a "pretty" face, but it was strongly molded and so full of character as to be arrestingly interesting. No one would ever forget his relentless stare or his charming, boyish laugh. He was a creature of fascinating conflict, a rogue, a gallant. Sometimes she was sure she would never grow tired of looking into those crystal blue eyes.

"My grandmother was angry with me because of you," he said.

"Why?"

"Because she thinks I dragged a naive, sweet innocent into the woods to lure into a dishonorable situation."

"Oh." Startled by the honesty of his reply, Whitney stopped to adjust a boot, lowering her hair over her eyes as she moistened her lips for her next question.

"How did you convince her that that wasn't the case?"

Eagle shrugged. "I didn't. Believe it or not, we live by high moral codes. She saw you — I would never be able to convince her that I wasn't after that shapely little body!"

"So?"

"So what?"

"So why isn't she angry anymore?" Whitney persisted with exasperation.

"Oh, that 'so.'" He stared at her again with a brow twitched high in cynical amusement. "I told her I was going to marry you at the Corn Dance."

"*What?*" The shout erupted incredulously from Whitney.

His eyes hardened and narrowed a fraction. "Don't worry about it — the ceremony won't be legal to you. You won't be obligated in any way."

Whitney realized her jaw was hanging open when she attempted to speak. Closing it, she moistened her lips. "Would you mind telling me what the hell the Corn Dance is and what type of illegal ceremony you think you're going to coerce me into?"

"As I said," he replied coolly, "it won't really affect you. And don't pull that indignant, affronted-maiden bit on me. I've discovered you have more than a bit of the teasing vixen in you, and if you persist in provoking me far enough, I'm sure that I can discover some real savage in myself and knock that royal superiority right off your sweet face."

"Why you — you arrogant brute!" Whitney hissed, clenching her fists tightly by her side as rage engulfed her. A saving grace of prudence kept her from tackling him. She was learning certain lessons.

"Watch that forked tongue," Eagle warned grimly, his stance as tense as hers. "Don't count on my not losing my patience. I have my limits, too, Whitney."

"Damn you!" Whitney swirled around and slammed her fist into a pine. She had to hit something!

"Smart move," Eagle drawled lazily. "There is hope for you."

Crooking her elbow, Whitney lowered her head onto it and leaned against the pine, striving for composure. In a muffled voice she politely demanded, "Would you please explain this Corn Dance ceremony to me? I know you like to be secretive, but I do believe I have a right to know certain things, since you plan on my participation."

"Witty and sarcastic still," Eagle commented assessively, "but the language and phrasing are much improved. The Corn Dance is one of a few remaining rituals to survive the times. It takes place once a year, and major tribal decisions are made and domestic matters handled. The Miccosukees seldom break the white man's laws, and our law is recognized within the tribe and the state. The date of the Corn Dance is kept a secret; very few outsiders are ever privileged to attend. As it happens, the Corn Dance begins tomorrow. If you are really interested in the tribe, you should count yourself lucky. You're being given a golden opportunity."

"Talk about people who think they're superior!" Whitney muttered caustically. "You'll pardon me if I don't kiss your feet for this golden opportunity! I want to understand a little more about this. You actually had the audacity to tell your grandmother you were marrying me at this — this war party? I thought Miccosukees didn't lie."

Eagle rubbed his temple patiently, and she could see clearly that he was in the mental process of counting to ten. "It is not a war party; it is the Green Corn Dance and it dates back to the festival held by our Georgia Creek ancestry. I did not lie to my grandmother. I have every intention of going through with the ceremony, and I can't see any reason it should annoy you to humor an old woman."

"Humor an old woman!" Whitney shrieked. "You want me to take part in a farcical marriage in front of some totem pole — "

"No totem pole," Eagle interrupted irritably. "We are the Seminole Nation and this is the Florida Everglades, not the Great Plains. Really, Whitney, you have to stop thinking that all Indians are painted savages who ride around on pinto ponies."

Whitney ground her teeth together and glared at him coldly. "I do know where I am." Pushing herself from the tree, she squared her shoulders and started back down the path.

"Get back here!" he growled with menace, spinning her around curtly with a clamped grip on her wrist. "You are not walking back to that encampment and up-setting my grandmother."

Whitney met his darkly challenging eyes for a minute, then shifted her gaze to her wrist. "I have no intention of upsetting Morning Dew," she told him, hoping her voice held no quaver.

"Fine. Then walk back with me nicely." His fingers interlaced with hers firmly and he strolled ahead of her. It was a small gesture, but it left Whitney seething. He thinks he's got it all sewn up, she thought angrily.

"You should like the festivities," Eagle said cheerfully as they neared the chickees. "It will be a chance for you to socialize with many clans and" — he gave her a glance of wriggled-brow mockery — "it will keep us both occupied so that we're not tearing at each other's hair."

"Black clouds do have silver linings," Whitney said through gritted teeth.

Their conversation was cut off, as Morning Dew had seen them and was wav-ing happily. The majority of her affection was oddly lavished on Whitney rather than her grandson. Whitney decided with a great deal of satisfaction that the stern old woman was on her side and still annoyed with White Eagle. Breaking into fast-clipped speech at their approach about how worried she'd been, Morning Dew came to her, slid an arm around her shoulder and led her to the cooking fire. Whitney sat as beckoned, looking at Eagle innocently.

"It seems you found yourself a fan while I was gone," he said briefly.

Whitney could not prevent a smug smile of satisfaction from curling her lips even as she lowered her head to hide it.

The meal was strangely peaceful and pleasant; the stew Eagle had referred to delicious. After the food had been consumed, Morning Dew served aromatic coffee in large ceramic mugs. The scent of the fresh brew reminded Whitney that she hadn't had a cigarette for hours. Eagle had been right; she had actually been too busy to miss the nicotine, but now she longed for a relaxing cigarette.

"I'll get them for you," Eagle said, reading her thoughts with a grin as he followed her eyes to the left chickee, where she had stowed her things.

"Thanks," she murmured.

Morning Dew began to pick up after the meal while he was gone, and when Whitney attempted to help, she was firmly motioned to sit. This night she was a guest. As soon as Eagle returned, Morning Dew spoke to him quickly, said good night to Whitney and left them.

Eagle lit a cigarette and handed it to Whitney as he sank back down beside her. "We'd better get to sleep soon ourselves," he remarked casually. "Our days are long."

Whitney inhaled deeply, annoyed to find her fingers shaking. The whole thing was so incongruous! Twenty-four hours ago she had met him; they were attracted with the force of magnetic poles, yet they clashed like a thunderstorm and argued with the ferocity of cats and dogs.

And here they were sipping coffee in the outlands of the Glades and casually discussing bedtime.

Crushing her cigarette carefully, Whitney finished her coffee with a quick gulp, yawned and stretched. There would be safety in sleep.

"You're right; these days are long," she said nervously. "Sleep sounds good." She started across the moonlit clearing and then hesitated. "Are you coming?"

"In a minute. My grandmother left you a present — you'll find it with the bedding."

Eagle spoke to her absently, as if his thoughts were far away. Shrugging, Whitney hurried over to their chickee and climbed up to the platform. The sleeping quarters, she knew, were high off the ground for security from snakes and other pests, just as the cooking house was built on a space of flat ground to avoid fire. She had learned during dinner that the Seminoles and other southeastern Indians had originally built log cabins, but due to their flight into the Glades and repeated attacks by a government determined to rout them, they had adapted to the thatched-roof homes.

Whitney prepared their bedding with surprising ease. Rather than the misery she had expected, the abode provided ample comfort. Mosquito netting kept the insects at bay, and thick quilts made the platform mattress undeniably soft. Straightening a cover, Whitney found the present Eagle had spoken of.

It was a sheer white gown, floor length and intricately and lovingly hand-sewn: a bride's gown.

Whitney stared at the beautiful costume for a minute of touched amazement; then her temper began to rise. Morning Dew had offered her nothing but kindness, and the old woman was being horribly deceived. How could her own grandson do such a thing to her!

"What's wrong? Don't you like it?"

Eagle had silently pounced onto the platform and now stood looking at her, his eyes curiously glittering in the gentle glow of fire and moon.

"Like it?" Whitney grated. "I like it just fine! But I have no intention of accepting such a gift. What you are doing to that woman is criminal!"

"I'll worry about my own actions," Eagle told her curtly, checking the nets as he once again began doffing his clothes. Fuming, Whitney discarded her boots and curled onto the floor-bed, her eyes tightly closed. He was calmly stripping with the same thoughtless abandon as before, but she certainly wasn't joining in a second time. The results of the first were still shatteringly fresh in her mind.

A moment later Eagle joined her, his length inches from her own. He was silent for so long she was sure he slept; then he spoke harshly in the darkness. "You're being ridiculous."

"About what?"

"Do you really think one or a hundred garments would stop me if I decided to attack your precious body? Don't flatter yourself that you are such a prize, and don't deceive yourself into thinking you don't want me. You were mine for the taking from the moment we met." The low gravel sound of his voice increased as he spoke. "But don't worry — I taunted you for a reaction this morning. If you leave these woods, you owe me nothing. If you stick to your part of the bargain, you'll still receive whatever assistance I can give you." He rolled away from her. "I'll even try to forget that you think we're all a pack of barbarians."

"But I don't!" Whitney protested.

"No?" He swung back and challenged her with remote curiosity. "Then just what is your problem?"

"I — I — I — "

"Un-unh!" he exclaimed impatiently. "For once, just talk. Try being a little honest with yourself."

Shivering in the moonlight, Whitney stared miserably into his searching eyes. How could she explain what she didn't understand? Suddenly his hand was on her cheek, his thumb caressing her smooth skin. With rough tenderness he traced a pattern down and across her lips, a hard look of longing tautening his features. She read physical desire in his tense demand, but it was coupled with something else — evidence that that desire could only be appeased if it was reciprocated.

Swallowing, Whitney closed her eyes, shivering but unprotesting. His lips found hers and cajoled sweetly until her mouth opened and offered and received. The seeking, stabbing warmth of his commanding tongue was easily drugging her into submissive euphoria again; his whisper-light touch upon her body was a magic she had long anticipated but never expected to experience. The natural masculine scent of him came to her with its intoxicating woodsy aroma, and she lifted her hands to touch the raven hair, the rippled golden muscles of his shoulders. Her shivers became shudders of awed excitement, and a low moan escaped her throat as his lips left hers to travel down the line to her breasts as he began to unsnap the buttons of her shirt slowly, one by one by one, his tongue making little darting forays of moistness upon her flesh.

His fingers slipped into the waistband of her pants, and while they assuredly found the button, he met her heavy-lidded gaze with eyes smoldering gray from the intensity of his desire. Their locked stare sent another heat wave of shivers coursing through her, and even as he watched her, his breath coming in deeper and deeper pants, she heard the slow, steady sound of her zipper sliding open to his gentle, determined insistence.

His eyes continued to hold hers as his lips came back to drink more fully of her mouth, and his fingers splayed over her hip and the skin of her upper abdomen, conquering the area newly exposed to his touch, easing the material firmly lower. Her fingers had clung to his back, then frozen; his free hand rose to catch her right one, guiding it along his length to his hip, to the rigid tautness of his stomach, to the intimate warmth of pulsating strength that was shockingly vibrant and alive. . . .

Whitney gasped, and then the panic set in. She felt innate terror that she couldn't possibly handle or please a man of such demanding virility. Her body went rigid, her moan became a fervent denial. Releasing him as if she had been burned, she pushed at his massive shoulders, pushed fiercely upon his broad chest.

Eagle jerked away from her, and his face was a basilisk of dark anger. With a muttered oath he sprang to his feet and impatiently stepped into his jeans, yanking them over his long legs in a furious motion.

Tears were forming in Whitney's eyes. "Where are you going?" she asked quickly, before he could hear the thickness in her voice.

"I'm taking my undesirable presence out to the alligators," he retorted, his eyes blazing and his mouth a grim white line. A second later he swung off the platform and was gone into the night.

CHAPTER FIVE

Stunned, Whitney stared after him as the seconds ticked by. He was gone, her mind kept repeating numbly. He thought she delighted in tormenting him, then calling a halt. He thought she would only tease and withdraw because he was unworthy of her. . . .

And still he would walk away before he would hurt her. . . .

Suddenly she couldn't bear his believing that her behavior was spawned by such motives. She couldn't define her feelings, she only knew that if he walked away tonight, she would lose something special, something that she craved desperately, needed. The void of his absence was already ripping apart her heart and soul.

Talk, he had told her. She didn't know what to say, but if only she could find him, the words would have to come. She had so terribly much at stake!

Scrambling to her feet, she hesitated. The hand-sewn gown lay strewn at the foot of the bedding. Whitney impulsively pulled off her clothing, ripping at the pearl snaps in her haste, and quickly put on the white gown. A supple swing brought her to the ground, and she peered anxiously down the pine path to the lake. Was that the way he had gone? A wraith in white beneath the moonlight, Whitney started down the path, terrified but determined. The trees, which offered gentle shade in the daytime, were a sinister refuge for macabre creatures in the night.

She started running as she neared the lake, praying that he would be there, praying that he wouldn't reject her. She stumbled from the trees and a sob escaped her as she fell to her knees before the water. He was there, sitting on the rock, watching the moon play on the water.

"Whitney!" He was beside her in a second, drawing her protectively to his side, his anger erased by concern. "What happened? What's wrong? Are you hurt? My grandmother — "

"No, no," Whitney gasped, burrowing her face in his neck. "Nothing is wrong, nothing happened. Morning Dew is fine. I — I wanted to talk to you, and I frightened myself in the trees."

"Oh." She felt his chest contract as he expelled a breath of relief. Then his hands were over her head, crushing the soft wings of her hair as he tilted her face upward. "What did you want to say that was so important?"

Whitney's mind went blank and she watched him with dismay. She had to talk or he would completely lose patience with her! "I don't know where to begin," she murmured unhappily.

"They usually do suggest that you begin at the beginning," Eagle said with a gentle grin. "Let's sit by the shore. Maybe if you watch the water, it will help."

He led her to the water's edge and they lowered themselves to the grass and sand shore. The effect *was* lulling, Whitney thought, as she cast her eyes over the luminescent star glow of the water. Eagle was beside her, but he didn't touch her. He was quiet, watching the water also, waiting with soothing patience. Whitney glanced at him, then returned her stare to the water.

"You really don't understand — "

"I want to," he interrupted softly.

"My problem isn't you; it's me. I would be a liar to deny I felt an immediate attraction to you. I'd also be a liar to say I've some-times thought you weren't . . . good enough for me." Sucking in her breath to begin again, Whitney kept her eyes studiously in front of her. If she were to see his crystal gaze now, she would falter; she would not be able to go on. She was going to try to say things she had kept submerged from her own thoughts. "I — I think there is some-thing wrong with me, although I don't know what a technical definition would be. I did-n't know it until I was married. I guess I ex-pected to get something out of sex, and then — then Gerry — my husband . . ." Whitney broke off, crunching her lip.

"Damn the man!" Eagle exclaimed, his anger a raw thing, explosive. "What did the bastard do to you? Did he hurt you, Whitney?"

Whitney glanced at him quickly with sur-prise. "Oh, no!" she explained quickly. "Gerry isn't a bastard. He's a very nice man. He never even raised his voice to me. It was-n't that . . ."

Eagle's dark brow knitted high above his eyes. She was trying; she was really trying. Breathing deeply to hold his impatience and perplexed curiosity in check, he told himself he must speak and move very slowly. She had to be led along on a very tender line.

"What then, Whitney?" His voice was nothing more than a soft urging on the breeze.

Her eyes flashed to his apologetically. "I guess I was brought up to be the Miss Virginia you tease me about. My entire life was set up for me. I went to private schools, then the University of Virginia. When I graduated I fell in with what was expected of me. Gerry was — and still is — my father's law partner. He came from a 'good' family, too. He's almost twenty years older than I am, but no one ever thought anything of that. He would be a good husband, father and provider. He belonged to all the right clubs; he sailed, played tennis and golf." Whitney lifted her hands helplessly. "I don't think I was ever in love with him, but I did care a great deal about him, and according to the old Southern aristocracy, love can grow if the elements are right . . ." There was a stick on the shore, and Whitney began to draw lines in the dirt as she settled her chin on her hugged knees. "This is what I'm not sure how to explain. I was always overly protected, so Gerry was, of course, my first real sexual experience. I was young, and I guess I was a romantic. I thought Gerry would adore me and we would create skyrockets together. Then that first night — " Whitney shuddered and stopped.

Eagle was ready to pull his own hair out. Instead he put a tender arm around her shoulders and lightly stroked the wispy wings of her hair. "What happened that first night?"

Whitney opened her mouth, but nothing came.

"Tell me, Whitney," Eagle urged sternly.

Somehow, in spite of sputtering, stopping and beginning again out of sequence, Whitney finally managed to explain. She told him how horrified her husband had been to find her eager to explore her sexuality, how seldom he had touched her, how they had only made love in the dark while remaining partially clothed. If she ever made a sound, he would turn from her, appalled, revolted.

"I — I always displeased him," Whitney finished awkwardly. "And I guess that's what so terrifies me now."

Eagle shook his head incredulously. "It's unbelievable."

"I wouldn't go through this to lie," Whitney strangled out, blinking furiously. Had she unburdened her heart and soul only to be ridiculed?

"No, no, little rabbit," he said with a smile, leaning back onto the earth and pulling her with him. "That's not what I meant at all! I don't believe a man could have you and not worship all that sexy beauty!" He was staring at her kindly, his blue eyes orbs of tender concern, his lips a twitch of sensuous relief. When he spoke, his voice was husky, a tone that sent quivers racing into her blood.

"Do you trust me?" he demanded suddenly, his touch still light.

Her eyes were wide in the moonlight, her answer a silken sigh. "Yes."

He spoke to her for a long, long time in that husky velvet voice before he began to make love to her. He told her that it pleased him just to see her, that she was built like a mythical goddess of love, that her hips and thighs were slender perfection, her breasts flowers of sensuality that begged to be touched. As he talked, his jeans were again cast aside, and he very gently pulled the white gown from her body.

"Look at me," he commanded as he lay his flesh against hers and she fluttered her lashes. "Look at me, Whitney." His features were incredibly tense with desire, but he smiled even as his eyes blazed.

"There is no way, sweet thing, that you could possibly displease me," he said, his voice becoming a harsher and harsher rasp. "And I want to hear you, my darling. I want you to touch me, I want you to forget everything except what you feel and I want you to scream if you feel like it . . ."

Whitney obediently kept her eyes open, locked with his in a tremulous hypnotism. His hand began a play upon her flesh as he continued to whisper in increasingly ragged breaths just how beautiful she was. His touch was very slow, very tender and yet masterful. His fingers traced lightly over her skin, drawing her with infinite finesse into his web. An instinctive reflex brought her hand to stop his as he caressed the rose-hued peaks of her nipples, but he deftly changed position and anchored her arms. His gentle play continued with stern control; his hands went on to explore fully the contours of her hips, her abdomen and the tender flesh of her inner thighs. Again reflex caused her to tense her slender legs together. "Trust me, Whitney," he murmured.

And she did. Teetering on the fine border-line between abandon and fear, Whitney crashed wildly into total submission as his seduction took an abrupt change and became demanding and urgent. His lips claimed hers with a fervency that left her breathless. His fingers deserted their eloquent teasing to plunge and exquisitely torture the tender, sensitive secrets of her flesh. A gasped moan escaped her, and Eagle replied with unbridled passion.

"Don't stop it, darling, don't stop it. Tell me . . . Touch me . . ."

Tentatively, hesitantly, she began to touch him. The shudders her fingers caused him excited her further and further until she was lost in a wonderful new world of exotic ecstasy. Hot kisses rained over her entire body, following the trails blazed by his knowing fingers. Enveloped in whirling, roller-coaster passion, Whitney writhed uncontrollably, arching into his glorious heat, straining wildly to give the erotic pleasure she received. She died a thousand little deaths.

"Eagle!" Her plea was a tormented whisper.

"Tell me!" he demanded, "Cry it out. Let me know."

"Oh, Eagle," she countered breathlessly. "I want you. I want you so very much . . ."

He filled her, he ignited her, he took her with the devastating passion she craved, his rhythm ever increasing with each new level of consuming exhilaration. And all the while he whispered, groaned, shuddered, driving her ever upward. They were locked together as one; Whitney's fingers dug desperately into his back, then a moan tore from her throat, a cry that was his name, an echo of the unleashed ecstasy that surged through her with a final convulsive, sweetly delicious tremble. The urgent passion subsided slowly, slowly, to be replaced by a feeling equally cherished. In that moment Whitney gave herself to him completely and was filled by him in a way that inexplicably bound her to him forever. Later she would have to think, to reason, to make light of her own fantastic thoughts, but for now she wore his brand, she could still relish in the scent of his body on hers; she was simply, irrevocably, in the most elemental of male-female responses — his.

Eagle shifted himself beside her and raised his head while he bent an elbow so that he could look at her again. In the aftermath of the intensity of their union, her damp body glistened in the moonlight, and he shook his head slightly to himself as he marveled at the perfect, cream beauty of her form. Her breasts rose and fell with the depth of her breathing, emphasizing the lovely contours and hollows of her collarbone and tightly flat abdomen. Her hair splayed in a wild fan beneath them both, while the fluffed wings framed her face in delicate curls. Heat filled him again as he watched her, and burning tenseness constricted within him. Drawing a finger down the line between the curves of her breasts to her navel, Eagle was consumed by emotions very similar to hers, and even more untamed. It was irrational, he knew, but he felt fiercely and unrestrainedly possessive. Irrational be damned! He would have her over and over again, he and only he. . . .

Her eyes flew open at his touch, and she smiled shyly.

"Skyrockets?" he inquired.

"And fireworks," she admitted.

He smiled in return, but his voice was grave as he curled a lock of her hair tenderly around his finger. "No more fears, Whitney? That husband of yours was the wrong one, you know. Do you believe me?"

"Yes."

"You are the most exquisitely pleasing creature I have ever known."

She couldn't reply to that. Did he mean it? Or was he bolstering her confidence? She wouldn't worry about it now . . . or wonder just how many "pleasing creatures" he had known. Lazy with satisfaction, she rolled into his chest and curled happily against it. Tonight was special. She didn't want to talk anymore; she had talked enough. For the moment nothing else mattered. She was wallowing in the satiated joy of lying next to the strength and power of this superbly created man. . . .

"No going to sleep on me!" he teased, nudging her. "Not here, anyway. I'm not that trusting of the snakes!"

As he had expected, the word "snakes" sent her flying to her feet. "You told me the lake was clear!" she accused in a wail.

"Well, it is, mostly. But I prefer to sleep off the ground — just in case!" He laughed, reaching for her hand. "Come on, sweetie, give an old man a hand up."

"Old man! How aged are you?"

"Three and a half decades come fall."

"I wouldn't have guessed you were a day over thirty-four."

"That's because Indians age well. Clean living, you know." Grinning, he collected her gown and his pants, then swung her dramatically into his arms. "This has always been one of my fantasies," he told her as she slipped her arms around his neck, "running naked through the woods with a captive woman. Have you ever seen yourself carried off like this?"

"No," Whitney said with a laugh. "And I don't know if it's such a hot idea now. Your grandmother could wake up — "

"My grandmother would love it. She's a true romantic — crazy about 'hot' ideas like this!"

In a few minutes they were back in the

chickee. As Whitney curled back into the covers with Eagle stretched beside her, contentment filled her. This bed in the woods was the most wonderful she had ever known. A belief in magic had been returned to her, and she was sailing on top of the world despite the crazy fact that she was falling in love with a man who would probably walk right back out of her life. . . .

Don't be silly, she chastised herself as she snuggled closer to him. She wasn't in love, nor was he. They had simply become "lovers." Odd terminology. . . .

She suddenly realized that Eagle was persistently touching her beneath the covers and that her body was automatically responding to his demands. "I thought we needed to get some sleep!" she teased, rubbing her cheek against his smooth chest.

"We do!" he whispered back. "I want to make sure we're really tired."

Whitney started giggling softly. Moon fever, she told herself.

"Stop that!" Eagle commanded, springing to pin her shoulders to their mat and to straddle her. "I taught you to moan, not laugh! I guess we have to refresh the lesson in your mind."

"Please," Whitney taunted with half-closed eyes. "I'm a slow learner."

"No, little witch," Eagle returned, his stare growing dark and passionately hard, his voice throaty. "You learn with natural ease. If you grow much more proficient, you could become a lethal weapon. You could please me into an early grave. . . ."

Her giggles quickly became panted moans as he lowered his head and fastened his teeth lightly over a nipple to begin the exquisite torment all over again. Whitney's fingers raked into his blue-raven hair as she arched to meet his tantalizing lovemaking. A willing captive. That was her last coherent thought. She had indeed become his captive.

"Up, rabbit!"

She was awakened by a firm tap on the rear end, to find Eagle standing above her, fully clothed, his costume today a braided Seminole shirt. Blinking groggily, Whitney graced him with a reproachful stare. Even he would have to admit that the hour was uncivilized.

Completely stoic, he arched a hand over his eyes and gesticulated to the horizon. "Pink trails of dawn are now consumed by golden eye of rising sun. Time for dedicated squaw to move rear like willow and get with it!"

"You've been watching too many John Wayne movies," Whitney muttered in cynical reply. But the night had changed her, and she couldn't resist an impish smile. "Couldn't you go fight the cavalry late today? Surely Indians must get sick leave, too!"

"No, no sick leave, not today." Smiling in return, he bent to kiss her lips lightly. "We have a lot of preparation to do. The Green Corn Dance begins at sunset — and you become a bride by nightfall. Even in the civilized world women do not laze around on their wedding days."

A frown puckered Whitney's brow and the soft womb of pleasure she had felt at wakening drained from her. How could he still be insisting that they take it all like a tremendous joke? In her one day here she was finding great respect for Morning Dew and the Miccosukee tribe, and she didn't feel like mocking their customs. Eagle was a Miccosukee! And he had told her to trust him. To play games to such an extent seemed nothing short of callous.

"I don't want to go through with the ceremony," she said stubbornly, drawing the covers to her chin.

The light in his eyes immediately disappeared. "I told you," he said harshly, "you

141

won't have to consider any of it legal."

"That's not the point — "Whitney began. "Oh, never mind!" she interrupted herself. What *was* the point? That she was falling in love and didn't want any part of what she had to remember was a farce? "We'll go through with it. I don't ever seem to win an argument with you, anyway."

Eagle's face remained dark and hard even after her agreement. "Get dressed," he said curtly. "There is a lot to be done. I've brought you an Indian skirt and blouse set. I thought you might like to attend the day in customary style."

He was gone before she could think of anything more to say. Scrambling from the covers. Whitney found the outfit. It was as carefully sewn and edged and braided as the white bridal gown. Sighing, Whitney slipped into the comfortable, porous material. She was fascinated by the prospect of attending the Corn Dance, even if it did raise a few moral dilemmas. She would have days ahead of her to talk with White Eagle . . . and tell him what? I realize that I'm supposed to be the sophisticated one and that a night of love in the chickee does not signify eternal devotion, but I think you taught your lessons a little too well and . . . what? God, what did she feel for him? He was like a fever in her blood . . . undefinable.

Eagle was out of sight when she approached the *sofki* pot, but Morning Dew was busily bustling about. She greeted Whitney with a wide smile and a cup of coffee, then, pointing to the pot, told Whitney to eat.

It was some kind of porridge, Whitney realized as she scooped up a bowl, smiled and tasted it. Ugh. Still she kept the smile plastered on her face, not wanting to hurt her hostess's feelings. Must be something you have to acquire a taste for, she thought wryly, grateful that at least she had a decent cup of coffee.

The now-familiar calls of several Glades birds — herons, egrets and beautiful wood ibis — came to her as she sipped her coffee, and Whitney was again struck by the strange sense of peace one could absorb in the woody environment. Listening to the birds, watching the gentle sway of moss upon cypress, she began to feel languorous. One more cup of coffee and a cigarette and I'll get going, she promised herself. A quick dart back to the chickee and a trip to the coffee pot and she was all set, comfortably lodged before the cooking fire, her silver lighter flashing quickly as she inhaled deeply. Ahh . . . nicotine. A sip of invigorating caffeine, and then another inhalation of soothing smoke. . . .

"Oh!" she yelped, startled and dismayed as the cigarette was suddenly wrenched from her fingers. Turning baleful, indignant, then increasingly angry eyes, she saw that Eagle was tossing the remainder of her cigarette into the cooking fire, his face a closed, stoic mask.

"What the hell do you think you're doing?" she demanded, jumping to her feet and facing him with her hands on her hips. "We agreed that my personal habits were my own business — "

"And that they are," he retorted rudely. "But I also mentioned that you wouldn't have time to laze around all day with a cigarette. You've work to do. Now. We need corn ground before we leave."

Whatever happened to the tender lover who had cherished her through the night, Whitney wondered fleetingly. Then her anger replaced any other feelings. "Now?" she queried imperiously. She reached for her pack of cigarettes, coolly eyeing him, and slowly lit another, inhaling and exhaling as calmly as if she were sitting in an elegant bar with a piña colada in her left hand. "I'll be with you in five minutes," she said with icy dismissal, tossing her head as she reclaimed her seat by the fire.

"I said *now!*" Eagle repeated softly, bending over her to wrench the second cigarette away. As Whitney struggled in rebellious protest, he also secured the entire pack and the silver lighter.

Never before accosted by such a situation, Whitney gave vent to frustrated rage, screaming, "Give those back! You have no right! Damn you — "

Ignoring her tantrum, Eagle swung on his heel. "Go take over the corn grinding for my grandmother. If you're a good, productive girl, I'll give you a cigarette break before we leave."

For a fraction of a second Whitney stood stunned, astounded that he would dare dictate her behavior to such an extent. Then she flew after him and pounded on his back ferociously. Her anger began a climb to disastrous heights as she realized he was laughing, and the next thing she knew, he had dragged her from his back to the ground and pinned her beneath him. With one hand he effortlessly secured both of hers over her head, grinned evilly and held the pack in front of him, pretending to muse seriously over the situation. "If I break them one by one," he said slowly, "you won't have any left!"

"No!" Whitney breathed.

"No what?" Eagle demanded.

Whitney broke into a string of abusive language she hadn't been aware that she knew.

"Un-huh, un-huh!" Eagle warned, clicking his teeth reproachfully.

Helpless with him above her, Whitney could not, nevertheless, control her temper. Wild rage decreed that she pit her entire strength against him, and she did so, writhing desperately against his weight and boalike grip on her wrists.

"Hmmm . . ." was his only response, his eyes assuming a brilliant twinkle. "That feels great. I think I like you mad."

"Ohhh," Whitney groaned, gritting her teeth. But he was right, the grinding of their hips together was bringing back memories of last night when they had joined together. . . .

"Let me up!" she demanded quickly, "and I'll go pound your damned corn or whatever it is you want done!"

Smiling, he came to his feet and helped her up. "Now that's the spirit! Whoever said that nicotine addiction couldn't be a good thing? You're going to want that cigarette so bad you'll just plow through the work!"

He chuckled as she stared at him furiously, her eyes snapping emeralds, her beautiful face taut with rebellion, her entire body seething. What perversity goaded him to provoke her, he wondered. Maybe a hint of the arrogance she accused him of. He really didn't give a damn about the corn himself . . . but watching her before the fire had reminded him too clearly that she had no part of this world that he could never really leave behind. She had become a wanton in his arms, instinctively pleasing him as no other woman, however well versed in the arts, ever had. He wanted to grab her and force her back to the chickee, or to a bed, or, hell, on the ground — anywhere. He wanted to take her and take her and take her until she was so indelibly bound to him and filled by him that she would never think of touching another man. . . .

That thought — a vision of her in the arms of another man, touching him, her lips upon him — sobered Eagle. He had only the next few days . . . just a few more days to possess and win her completely.

"Well, go on!" he growled abruptly, unable to control the forces that gripped him like a madman. Elemental power was all that he had.

She spun past him, muttering about what he was beneath her breath. Brute. Domineering. Uncouth. He even rated

147

"chauvinist." Her hips swayed enticingly as she walked away. "Damnit!" was the last thing he heard her murmur.

The corn grinder was simply a section of large log, fashioned with a hollow to hold shelled corn. The corn became pulverized by the dropping of a heavy wooden pestle.

Whitney's arms were aching within a few minutes, but her anger kept her moving. Morning Dew helped her, instructing her in the easiest way to control the heavy pestle. Then she was on her own. Everyone in the village was busy preparing supplies for the festival.

When she had finally finished with the offending corn, Whitney realized it couldn't be more than nine A.M., yet she felt as if the day should be over. Anyway, she certainly deserved her break! Strolling back to the cooking fire, she found hot coffee and her cigarettes. Wary lest Eagle come upon her and decree that she was supposed to have scrubbed the dirt floor, Whitney took her coffee and cigarette through the little alcove in the trees that led to the lake, found a level stump and sat to enjoy her brief spell of relaxation. God, but she hurt all over! And she was one hell of a fool. What was possessing her to stay and endure such treatment? The answer came to her immediately. Eagle. She *was* possessed.

A smile twitched her lips. So she was going to become his bride tonight! He would certainly be sorry he had been so rough on her. The continually joked about excuse of a headache had to be a frequent reality for an Indian wife. Headache, nothing! Everything that was part of her ached!

"I'll have you grind the corn more often if it makes you this happy!"

Whitney glanced from the smoke of her cigarette to Eagle, who had come upon her with his usual irritating silence. A smart retort died in her throat as she stared at him.

He was still clad in the richly colorful Seminole shirt, but he had added to his native costume. His dark head was adorned by a turban of white egret feathers and a warlike band of silver encircled his neck. He had shed his jeans for the brief "skirt" of the kind the Seminoles wore hundreds of years ago, and his high boots were now of buckskin. A knife was strapped to one thigh, and he carried a large, lethal-looking bow, while arrow points peeked over his shoulder. Surely, Whitney decided, Osceola himself had never looked so awe inspiring and fearsome when he arrogantly turned down any terms of peace. Through the decades Eagle had inherited the structure and aura of relentless pride, of independence, of stubborn, ruthless willpower. The bright blue of his eyes and the gauntness of his high-boned face gave conclusive evidence of his white heritage, but that merely seemed to accentuate the ruggedness of his chosen native stance.

"You might want to shut your mouth," he suggested blandly, a spark of humor discernible in the wry twist of his lips. "You could trap a mosquito if you're not careful."

Whitney snapped her mouth shut. "You look . . . uh . . . you look . . ."

"Barbaric?"

Whitney shook her head. "No," she said softly. "Regal. Like a chief. Are you a chief?"

"No," he replied, joining her on the stump. "We don't have chiefs these days. We have council members."

Speaking her thoughts aloud, Whitney continued. "Well, you do look just like I picture Osceola to have looked."

Eagle laughed aloud easily, but Whitney felt comfortable with the pleasant sound. Reaching over his shoulder into the leather satchel that held his arrows, he said easily, "Here — I brought you your cigarettes."

"Thanks," Whitney replied sardonically. "I just smoked one." Then, realizing she might be put on another "cold turkey" spell, she accepted the pack from him and lit up. He started to laugh again and she tweaked an inquiring brow at him.

"*You* look like one of those feminist cigarette ads! Old-fashioned dress from head to toe, hiding away in the bushes to smoke!"

"Aren't you glad I'm not a real women's libber? I'd never be in these woods!"

His light banter ceased suddenly and he took her chin gently in his hand. The timbre of his voice was soft and low. "What are you, Whitney? What are you really?"

"I don't know what you mean," she replied, annoyed that her answer warbled nervously. Their relationship was such a strange one. It was business between them, then hostility, then passion and chemistry. But passion was one thing in the throes of ecstasy in his arms; friendship was another. She was terrified to come too close, to put demands on an intimacy that he had probably shared before yet to her was . . . skyrockets.

He didn't release her chin, and his next question was blunt and audacious. "Were you divorced because of the sex problem? Don't start blushing — after last night it's a little late for secrets or hedging with me."

Whitney managed to extract her chin on

the pretense of taking a drag of her cigarette. Staring straight ahead of her, she honestly replied. "No. I didn't even realize at the time that I was missing anything. We just made each other miserable. I wanted to work; Gerry wanted a wife who was always home looking pretty. He wouldn't force me to quit, and I couldn't volunteer. One day I just sat down and told him that what we were doing was ridiculous. We were — and are — friends. We wanted different things, that's all."

The tiny alcove seemed very hushed when she finished speaking. Eagle eventually asked, "And what is it that you want?"

"I don't know exactly," Whitney answered truthfully. "To be respected, I suppose. To have my opinions matter. To care deeply . . ." She crushed her cigarette, very carefully grinding it into the dirt. "What do you want out of life?"

"Probably the very same things," he answered her levelly, his blue eyes warmly sincere for the moment. "I think we all do."

He stood abruptly, and the close intimacy was broken. "Come, Whitney. Your dugout awaits."

Whitney rose obediently and placed her hand in his outstretched one. They were both guarded again, and yet something more had been forged between them than the chemistry that had promised that they would be lovers just as surely as the sun would rise.

But, Whitney thought wryly, just as surely as that sun would rise, the moon would follow. They were both willful, stubborn and demanding. They would love, but would they hate with equal depth and ferocity?

As the dugout trailed through the marshy land to take them to the Green Corn Dance, Eagle explained something of the festival. The majority of the Miccosukees in Florida would attend, even those living in more northern parts of the state. Although the Muskogee or Cow Creek Seminoles held their own dance, many of them would also come. Many ancient customs would be adhered to, and many men, who usually wore jeans these days, would dress in tribal costume. The Indians hunted with shotguns; the bow and arrows he carried were for games, although they were not a competitive people. The idea of a contest was not to win but to excel as far as one could for one's own benefit and satisfaction. The good of the family and tribe was the main consideration for all Seminoles. "Actually," Eagle said with a grin, "we don't call ourselves Seminoles; in

Muskogee we are *Istichatee,* in Miccosukee, we are *Yakitisee.* Both terms mean 'red people.'"

"I hope I remember all this!" Whitney said, watching the strong play of muscles in his arms as he unerringly guided the dugout canoe that carried the two of them and Morning Dew with fixed precision through what appeared to be endless miles of identical marshland. "And I do hope that the venerable J. E. Stewart is impressed!"

If she hadn't been preoccupied with her own thoughts, Whitney might have noticed that Eagle grimaced ruefully. As it was, she frowned and continued in the same vein. "Although I'm still at a loss as to what I should be understanding. From what I've learned, the Indians do live hard lives! Think how much easier life could be for your grandmother if she had a washing machine and electricity and — "

"Have you been unhappy, Whitney?"

The question interrupted her with a hushed, sensual quality. Blushing, Whitney trailed a hand over the top of the water and whispered, "No." Then she raised her eyes to his with timid mischief. "But you can be pushy at times! Argumentative and demanding!"

He smiled rakishly in return. "That's

right. When one deals with a dedicated re-former, one must be prepared to demand."

Before Whitney could think of a suitable reply, Eagle pointed over her shoulder with a paddle. "Ceremony grounds."

Ceremony grounds! Whitney groaned, twisting to see the mass activity. There had to be close to a thousand Indians. A faint, tremulous fear edged over her.

Fortunately she didn't have long to dwell on her sense of uneasiness. The gathering was a social occasion, and they were shortly bustling through crowds with greetings being called all around them. Makeshift chickees had been arranged by each family, and along with the other Eagles, they were soon settling into their clan sector. Whitney was turned over to Morning Dew for the afternoon, since Eagle was called upon to join with his male peers for certain func-tions. Whitney rather sullenly let it be known that she didn't particularly approve of such sexism.

"Don't pout!" Eagle said with a laugh. "Our women run the domestic activities — heredity is matrilineal. It has only been in the last century that we have begun to take our fathers' names — and that because of white influence." Suddenly he grasped her tightly to him and whispered, "And that, darling, is why it shall be to my mother's ancestral home that I bring my bride this evening for her nuptials."

His voice held threat; it held promise. A quivering of anticipation made Whitney loath to move her face from the harbor of his chest. He taunted her, and yet he - enthralled her. She should be denying the hypocrisy of the farce, but she couldn't. She was waiting for the night and a Miccosukee blessing of their strange union.

It wasn't long in coming. Morning Dew spent the afternoon entertaining various of her women friends. Some of the conversations were in the Miccosukee tongue, with Morning Dew translating for Whitney, and she was affectionately drawn into the circle of women who blatantly studied her, but did it with such warmth, interest and sincerity that she could feel no resentment. It was touching to see the pride Morning Dew exhibited in her, heart-warming and painful. But Whitney was obsessed by the evening; she couldn't and wouldn't put a stop to the events that were due to occur. She had been swept into a strange dream from which she had no desire to awaken.

Then the sun made its slow descent into the horizon. Whitney, bathed and dressed, her hair carefully braided, was led to the

156

center of the celebration, where a massive bonfire burned. Men and women were joining by the fire, and as Whitney watched, they began a dance. The music of a flute could be heard accompanying a slow chant, which was joined by the rattle of shells and the pulsations of drumbeats upon various devices.

Eagle, clad in a multitude of feathers that turbaned around his head, was among the dancers. For a moment his eyes locked with hers through the mystical orange glow of the firelight. They were brilliant, triumphant, exultant — and a shade devilish and wild. An ember of fear raged through Whitney, interrupting the trancelike quality of the dream she lived. What was she getting into? Three days ago the man staring at her with victorious possession had been unknown to her.

Eagle's view of her was whipped away as the dance increased in tempo, and Whitney was back in her trance. She didn't care. Past and future held no meaning. Whoever or whatever he was didn't matter. She wanted him with pure and unadulterated yearning and love. The trappings of the man meant nothing — he was the essence of all she had ever sought and desired in a male — a lover, a provider, a mate.

The dance ended. Suddenly Whitney became part of the activities — the main part. She was standing before the elders of the tribe and the councilmen and her tongue was unglueing to form alien syllables in repetition. Eagle was beside her; she was his. It was over, yet still the bonfire raged and the ancient hypnotism of the ritual remained. The dream would continue.

Only one incident occurred to remind her that she was still residing in the twentieth century. She was about to be led away for her "honeymoon" night when the head of the council, a weathered and stately old Indian man, kissed her cheek in a very Anglo fashion.

"Congratulations, my dear," he told her, his English enunciated in a clear, only slightly accented voice. "I hope you'll be very happy."

But Whitney had no chance to muse over his perfect use of her own language. She was taken to a secluded chickee in the shelter of warm, welcoming pines. She was left standing, a beautiful young bride, awaiting her husband, her noble warrior man.

CHAPTER SIX

She stood in ethereal splendor as he approached, a vision of spectral loveliness. The moonlight danced upon the dark waves of her hair, which had been loosened to form a glorious cloak around her shoulders. She was still, perfectly still, as if she didn't even breathe, and the glow upon her skin gave it the cast of silken cream alabaster. In the darkness her eyes were prisms of jade, bright and liquid against the whiteness of her face.

She didn't see him on the path, Eagle knew, and he allowed himself the luxury of simply watching her. He had no desire to rush anything. In his heart he would be claiming his bride, and despite all that he knew, all that had come before, she was defenseless and as tender as a trusting doe as she waited.

Her eyes came to his and he saw that they were tremulous, that a faint shivering held her body in its grip. He stared at her a moment longer, then slowly walked to her, his eyes never leaving hers. He moved like a panther in the night, his sleek muscles fluid, his steps sure. The passion that would be culminated had begun with that first searing eye contact, which had locked them together in a union beyond description but known to man since the beginning of time.

Eagle leaped to the platform with a muffled thump and stood just inches from her, inhaling the soft perfume of her femininity, absorbing the radiating warmth of her nearness. Tonight there was no need to talk. She was frightened, but willing and eager. It was all still new. Her eyes told everything.

His fingers trembled slightly as he moved them to unfasten the strings of the gown she wore. It fell to her feet in a soft rustle, and he drank in the beauty of her nakedness slowly with his eyes, worshipping her as he might a statue of the finest marble. But she wasn't marble, she was flesh and blood and her quivering form cried out to be touched as her eyes met his again with mute pleading.

Still, he could not rush. He brought his hands to her shoulders, slowly down the soft length of her arms, along the exquisite contours of her delicately molded back. His lips claimed hers, slowly, seductively, savoring each new depth of the warmth of her moist mouth. Heat grew within him, embering, flaring, yet he kept it within rigid control. His kisses blazed new trails from her mouth, down the swanlike length of her neck, onward across her breasts to tease, torment and demand upon the hard rosy peaks that rose instinctively to his touch against the firm roundness that arched into his hands. A famished man, his head swimming, he went on to thirst and thirst, tasting the taut flesh of her rib cage, the tiny indentation of her navel, the sweet, sweet skin of her abdomen and the soft skin that lurked below hiding all that was his. And all the while that he enticed, teased and cajoled, his own desire intensified like a tornado, spinning, whipping, spiraling as her quivers became sensuous undulations and her silence a series of moans and sighs that pleaded and demanded in return.

Then it was she who became the aggressor. No longer able to stand, she fell to her knees and buried herself against him. Their fingers worked together to cast aside his clothing, and she was drinking of his smooth, tight flesh, relishing the spasm of muscles beneath her lips and hands, drawing the same pleasure as he from the wanton excitement she elicited. She couldn't touch him, feel him, taste the fine salt of his body enough . . . nor could she satiate the appetite that raged like a bonfire, gnawing, creating a hunger as demanding and unquenchable as his.

A hoarse cry rumbled in the depth of his powerful chest, and the mute satisfaction of a woman who has equally seduced a man in loving torment mingled naturally into Whitney's primal level of ecstasy, spurring her still further into the realm of sensuous magic. Then it was he who commanded again, he who navigated her writhing body, he who took her with a rough urgency that propelled them into shock wave after shock wave of ceaseless sweet pleasure until the unbearable exploded into a high of delicious fulfillment so wonderful that they floated in a land where time stood still until the crest washed back in a wave of complete, giving satisfaction.

They were silent again in the aftermath of the incredible maelstrom of their love-making. It wasn't a time to talk, Whitney thought dreamily, feeling the breadth of his chest expanding and contracting beneath the light touch of her slender fingers. It was a time to cherish sensations, to mindlessly enjoy all that had transpired and simply hold on to the beauty. With her head upon his shoulder, her arm casually slung over him, her body melded against his, she gave in to her euphoria and total physical and mental exhaustion. A final shudder rippled its way through her limbs; a long sigh of happiness whistled softly through her lips. She slept, in the peace and security that would envelope her wherever this man might be.

Eagle stared briefly at the moonglow through the trees. He was thinking about the future and the woman who was confidently coiled to his length — so fragile, so fine and yet so strong. And, for reasons of her own, she trusted him. He had taught her, but it was he, the teacher, who knew just how special and precious the ties that bound them were. He glanced tenderly at the face nestled in his shoulder. Her dark lashes swept her cheeks in sleep and her lips were prettily curved, even at rest. Tomorrow, he told himself. Tomorrow he would talk to her; he would explain what he had done. In that night he had learned the true meaning of his fanatical desire to possess her completely, and he was once more convinced that he would never let her go. Closing his eyes, he felt the perfect warmth of his discovery and the age-old, masculine, triumphant comfort of having his beautiful woman wedged to his strength. He slept, too, his lips curved into a smile with the satisfaction that she had come to him first in a bed in the woods.

It was the morning song of a chorus of birds that woke Whitney, a symphony that rang sweetly in the dew damp air. She listened lazily for a moment without opening her eyes, luxuriating in the fresh scent and feel of the new day — and in the contentment of languorous satiation that had stayed with her through the night. She was experiencing a rush of womanly wonder at the beauty of the world, awed that Eagle was beside her still, his male strength enveloping her fragility. . . .

He stirred beside her, and his eyes were sensuously heavy lidded as they met hers. In the night they had shifted, and he was leaning over her, his leg thrown casually over hers, his arm gently entrapping her breasts. He kissed her lips lightly, then reverently he kissed the tender peak of each mound beneath his arm's captivity. He smiled, and Whitney gently drew her knuckles over his cheek, smiling in return.

Something rustled in the bushes, and a look of alarm crossed Whitney's face. She automatically reached for the coverings, but his imprisoning arm held her firm.

"Just the birds," he murmured, "just the birds, my sweet." He chuckled and released her reluctantly to stand and rustle through their belongings. Whitney relaxed and narrowed her eyes to watch him through covert slits. He was incredible, she thought with smug, feminine satisfaction. Incredibly powerful, incredibly superb, incredibly masculine. It was marvelous just to watch the blending of sinewed muscles and tendons as he moved near, unconscious of the nakedness that was natural when he was with her.

He found a pair of briefs and jeans and stepped into them, pausing only for a second to glance at her with hesitant longing as she lay curled like a kitten near his feet, enticingly half covered. But the commotion of the birds was a warning that daybreak had come and a scurry of activity would shortly begin. Willpower snapped him from his enchanted reverie, and he pulled up the zipper of his snug jeans. "Let's take a walk," he suggested huskily.

Whitney grinned her agreement and stretched. "What about your costume today?" she asked.

He grimaced wryly. "There will be games and contests today — among them alligator wrestling." He raised a rueful brow and knelt back beside her, unable to resist the temptation to trace a finger down her curved, beautifully sculpted back to the tiny hollows that dimpled at its base. "Even those sworn to custom wear jeans for the alligators — they have fast-snapping, powerful jaws."

"You really wrestle alligators?"

"Ummmm," he smiled at the concern in her eyes and gave in to another temptation — that of drawing her from her cocoon of sheets and taking her into his arms. He allowed himself a drawn-out kiss while caressing her enticing body before pulling away with a shaky breath and handing her her clothing. "It's late."

"Telling time by the sun?" she teased, obediently dressing.

"As a matter of fact, yes," he retorted, grinning. "And I'll be ribbed mercilessly if we don't make an appearance soon, but I want to walk with you in a private fantasy for a while." Hopping lithely to the ground, he added, "Finish dressing, my love, and follow me. I won't lead you astray."

"Hah!" Whitney quipped, but she happily placed her hands upon his shoulders to leap to the ground with the assistance of his warm, muscle-corded arms. Snuggled to his side, she complacently followed his leading footsteps into the pines, content as he for

166

the moment to wallow in the exquisite beauty between them and around them.

It was a short nature hike. Eagle held her close to his beating heart while he shushed her and pointed out the precious foliage and creatures that created the one-of-a-kind paradise of the Everglades: rare flowers carried by ocean currents north from the tropics in ancient times when the land was forming, animals from the north that had adapted to the south, long-legged birds that added their pastel splendor to the darker wood hues.

Eagle held her still against him as they silently watched a great blue heron take flight in smooth majesty. His arms were circled around her waist, and his breath tickled her ear. "We have to get back," he said with a sigh. "'Gator time."

"You're serious."

"I'm serious." He laughed, taking her hand. "Come on!"

They retraced the pine trail back to the main ceremony grounds, where they approached an area of sturdy fencing where others were beginning to congregate.

"Be careful," she pleaded.

He gave her a thumbs-up sign. "I learned this from the best at seventeen — and I'm always careful!"

Whitney was then left as a spectator while Eagle joined the men for their exhibitions in the pit. She watched with fearful fascination as the men entered and maneuvered the animals skillfully — always careful, as Eagle had said — expertly watching while working to see that no opening jaws were behind them. The angry hissing increased as the prodded animals scampered for their reserves of water, moving with a startling speed.

"They can outrun a racehorse for a short distance, at sixty-five miles an hour," a friendly voice told Whitney.

"Randy!" she exclaimed happily, turning to see him with Katie Eagle.

"How are you enjoying the festivities?" Katie asked. "Randy and I are late because of some herd problems, but I hear my brother did connive you into the wedding my grandmother demanded."

"Ah . . . yes," Whitney murmured, turning her gaze back to the alligator pit. Eagle was entering, and she drew in a sharp breath.

"Don't worry," Katie said with a chuckle, "he knows what he's doing."

Apparently he did. Barefoot and barechested as the other men had been, Eagle held his pole and scampered around the creatures with cautious grace. He singled out his animal and drew it to the center by the tail. Then he had the jaws in a careful grip and performed the stunt of holding them closed against his chest by the strength of his chin alone. Finally he put the animal to sleep by rubbing sand on the pale underbelly.

"They fall asleep," Randy said, "because of the rush of blood from their tails to their heads. He won't leave it long, though — it could be harmful to the animal."

Suddenly Eagle was back with them. His words were for Katie; they were sharp and in the Miccosukee tongue. Katie seemed to deny something indignantly, and Eagle's voice began to soften. An apology? Whitney wondered. For what? He had gone into what seemed to be an explanation. Katie began agreeing with a soft smile that switched mischievously to Whitney. Whitney realized with sinking clarity that it all had something to do with the Miccosukee wedding. Katie and Randy had to know that it was a sham. A dizzying sensation froze Whitney. She didn't want it to be a sham. All morning she had walked beside him and talked with him in a lighthearted flippancy, one that bespoke of tender, reciprocated intimacy. She didn't want shades of reality intruding now.

But neither was she a fool. They were discussing her as if she weren't there, and she just wasn't going to have it. "Excuse me, you two!" she interrupted. "What's going on?"

She received a simultaneous pair of "nothings" that were riddled with guilt. Randy Harris looked at her uneasily. His eyes darted back to Eagle. "I hate like hell to come between 'newlyweds,'" he said hollowly, "but it seems to me we have to split up this party. I believe they're expecting you at the council meeting."

"Yeah . . . uh . . . yeah. . . ." Eagle murmured. He brushed his lips over Whitney's and gave her a warm smile. "Stick with Katie. I'll see you later." Raising his brows with a grimace, he added, "Tribal powwow, you know."

Randy and Eagle disappeared into the crowd that hovered around the pit, and Whitney looked at Katie. She had given Whitney answers before, and now she chatted like a magpie — about anything but her brother or their family. It would be useless to question Katie, Whitney shrewdly realized. She was thoroughly under Eagle's control.

Whitney wasn't sure that she wanted to question her, anyway. She had the intuition that knowledge would hurt her. Better to enjoy what was for her allotted time than to begin already to chastise herself for falling into the arms of a compelling man without having the sense to think about what she was doing.

Katie, relieved to find she wasn't going to be cross-examined, dropped her inane wanderings and suggested they join a game. It resembled lacrosse, and men and women were joining in alike, all in good spirits and camaraderie. Whitney protested that she would bring certain defeat to her team, but she was ignored and soon she was running through the field, laughing like a child. She knew surreptitious glances were often cast her way, and that they all wondered about the woman who had "married" Eagle. Did she read envy in certain eyes? She hoped so. She wanted to fit into this society, which had accepted her with warmth and sincerity.

Whitney didn't get to see much more of Eagle during the day and evening. The council meeting was long; there were many disputes to be settled. She ate with Katie, Morning Dew and other women of the Eagle family; then she was again a spectator of the all-male ritual of the "Black Drink." The Corn Dance, Katie explained, was a time to come back to the tribe, to reevaluate oneself and, in old times of battle, the *Asi* or Black Drink had been a war potion for the braves as well as a purifier. The men drank, cried to the spirits and danced. When the ritual was over, Eagle was again swarmed over by his peers, who seemed to have much to discuss. Whitney found herself returning to the Eagle camp with Katie to await her new husband's return.

The woods were ominous without Eagle. Whitney was a jumble of nerves, half afire for him with burning anticipation, half afraid of the night noises that she recognized yet still didn't trust — rustlings in the pines, the call of birds, . . . the soft note of a John Denver tune coming to her over the breeze.

John Denver! Whitney sat bolt upright, listening. Yes, she could hear a guitar and a singer with a pleasant tenor warbling a charming strain to "Rocky Mountain High." Who? Where? It was impossible! She couldn't be hearing what she was hearing — Denver music in the woods.

But she was.

And it wasn't an acoustical guitar she was hearing. It was definitely electric.

After a while the music ceased. Whitney lay her head back down, pondering the puzzle. But the days had been too much for her. She yawned, dozing into sleep despite her desires and fears. She would ask Eagle who had been the pleasant tenor, she decided. As soon as she saw him.

But electricity in the woods? Maybe she *had* imagined that . . . Eagle would explain.

But she never had a chance to ask him. When he returned she was aroused rather than awakened, and it was late in the night when she contentedly drifted into slumber again, her curiosity blissfully forgotten.

Whitney sat outside the chickee thinking of the night she had spent in Eagle's arms. If only she weren't so tired! The nights of wild exhilaration were wonderful dreams, but lack of actual sleeping hours was taking a toll. She was a woebegone sight as she sat before the chickee, her native costume bunched about her knees, her hair framing bright green eyes that peered above mauve shadows. She yawned with a shake of her head. How did Eagle do it? He had been up and gone before she had managed to blink.

"My goodness! Where did you come from?"

Whitney quickly glanced up from the ground where she had been drawing patterns with her finger to find herself facing a tall, slim man with a pleasant crop of neat, snow-white hair. He was dressed in a sedate three-piece suit of navy that was obviously well tailored. As she frowned at him with confusion, he smiled. The friendly grin that twisted his lips stretched to his eyes — eyes that were a brilliant, vivid blue.

Whitney scrambled to her feet, dusting her hands against her calico skirt. She knew she was staring rudely, but the resemblance was extraordinary. Extending her hand while she searched for her tongue, Whitney smiled. "How do you do?" she managed. "My name is Whitney Latham. Eagle — your son, I know he must be your son! — brought me out here. I am — I mean I was — am! — with T and C Development and he thought I might be interested in learning the real way of life of the Indians involved in our transactions. We met in the woods, you see . . ." How ridiculous she was sounding! Cool, poised Whitney Latham, who could face the presidents of multimillion-dollar corporations without the flicker of an eyelash! Why was she babbling before this dignified, friendly, middle-aged man?

Because he was her father-in-law and knew nothing of the bogus wedding? No; he wasn't really her father-in-law. But he was Eagle's father, that she knew beyond a doubt. And absurd as it was, she loved Eagle. She wanted so desperately to know his father . . . and her curiosity about his heritage was so strong that she couldn't possibly ask everything at once!

The man laughed, an easy, good-natured sound. "Slow down, Miss Latham. This is a most intriguing situation! You met — uh — Eagle, you say, in the woods. And he brought you out here?"

Whitney blushed slightly and explained how she had stumbled into the cabin off Alligator Alley. Lifting her hands in confused offering, she ended with, "So you see, Eagle thought I could best learn what I don't know by actually living it."

"And what has he been teaching you?"

"How to grind corn, prepare vegetables . . ."

The dignified old man with the beautiful, crinkling eyes interrupted Whitney's recital with laughter.

"Oh, I am sorry, my dear. Forgive me!" he begged, seeing her bewilderment. "That son of mine! What else has he been up to? Never mind, I think I have an idea. He has taken you for a real ride!"

Whitney smiled and attempted to sound nonchalant. "Oh? Please go on!" She forced the trembling that had assailed her to cease, and the look of confusion left her face as she gave him her most beguiling grin. "Perhaps I can take your son for a little ride in return!" Just right, she decided. She sounded like a female intent on a slight teasing revenge, not a woman ready to explode with rage and pain. Ride! she seethed inwardly. Ride! What kind of ride?

"Perhaps I'm being vague," the man said cheerfully, "but I'm not sure why my son brought you to his grandmother. You see the majority of the Indians today are educated and well aware of the offerings of our society. Several of the families run stores and businesses on the Trail. A number of the men and women hold jobs in the cities, such as in Naples, Miami and Homestead. If they want electricity they have it installed. If they want cornmeal, well, they usually buy it. Especially the younger crowd. Schools have exposed them to the niceties — and the headaches! — of civilization."

Denver, Whitney thought dully, that was why she had heard the John Denver music. That was why the head of the council had expressed his best wishes in English. They probably all spoke English, and she had played the complete fool. . . . "Do you mean," she began aloud, "that none of this is real?"

"No, no! Forgive me again! This is very real! Morning Dew is an old-time Miccosukee," he told her warmly. "This is her way of life. She desires no contact with so-called civilization. I'm shocked that she allowed Eagle to bring you here like this. How did he manage it?"

Whitney couldn't bring herself to mention the tribal wedding. She only hoped she could escape the gentle man before he discovered the extent of her relationship with his son. Escape! How? But she had to get away.

"I — I'm not sure," she whispered vaguely.

"How did Eagle con *you* into this?"

"He . . . uh . . . he promised to smooth things over for me with Jonathan Stewart."

It was the white-haired man's turn to look puzzled. "I don't understand, but I think I'd like to. Smooth what things over? You see, I am Jonathan Stewart."

Oh God! Whitney mutely groaned. Of course! That was the secrecy regarding his paternity! That was why Eagle was so sure he had all the influence he needed. "I don't see what you don't understand, Mr. Stewart," she began politely. "Surely you know you are due to meet with me next week on a solution to the land problem."

His brows raised in a high arch, so like Eagle's that a fierce stab of pain ripped into her heart. "You're to meet with me next week?"

"Yes, sir. With Mr. Jonathan E. Stewart."

"Oh, my dear Miss Latham! You *have* been taken for a ride, and I can see I'll be having a long discussion with my son! It isn't me that you're supposed to be meeting. I'm Jonathan Lee Stewart. You were destined to meet my son from the beginning — you merely came upon him prematurely. He is Jonathan E. Stewart. Eagle. Jonathan Eagle Stewart. The Miccosukees call him White Eagle because of me, his father."

Whitney had never fainted, but she was sure the blackness enveloping her would soon cause a hasty descent to the ground. Her knees buckled beneath her. "I think I'll sit for a minute," she said, and her voice had a buzzing quality as it came to her ears. How had she been so wretchedly stupid and naive? She had been baited — Miss Virginia, indeed! — and fallen hook, line and sinker for every deception dangled before her.

"Are you all right, Miss Latham?" Jonathan Stewart, his blue eyes pools of concern, knelt beside her, mindless of his impeccable suit in the earth.

"Fine. . . ." Whitney murmured faintly, dredging up a reassuring grin. Stewart seemed to think of it all as a friendly, harmless practical joke. But he didn't know how terribly involved it had been! He didn't know that his son had solicited her love and trust while subtly stabbing her in the back all the while! Oh, God! Whitney thought over everything that had happened in a flash in her mind, like the last visions of a drowning victim. Her demand to know if Eagle spoke English. Her often unintended and naive remarks about the Indians and their way of life. . . .

Yes, it had all been a plot to put her in her place. The tender passion of his lovemaking had been nothing but part of the plan. Lord! How he probably intended to laugh when she walked into his Naples office. . . .

He would never have the chance, Whitney determined, and the blackness that encompassed her became a brilliant white light of fury. Now it was her turn. She wasn't sure of her move yet, but she was getting out of these woods — without seeing Eagle again. She would face him in his Naples office — prepared!

"Miss Latham?"

"I'm fine — I really am!" Whitney assured the senior Stewart. "And please call me Whitney." There was no reason to hurt this kindly man because she was swearing vengeance on his son! "Tell me, sir, how do you happen to be out here?"

"That's easy," Stewart said as he grinned amicably. "I came because of Morning Dew.

I see her whenever I come to the South. I live in Chicago, and the one offering of civilization that Morning Dew appreciates is Fanny Mae candy." He patted his jacket. "I always bring her a box."

"Oh," Whitney murmured. "Then you have no problems finding this elusive Corn Dance?"

Stewart gave her another of his gentle smiles. "No. I am also an Eagle by marriage, and the Miccosukees know that I respect their privacy and culture. I lived with them many years."

"Yes . . . yes . . . of course," Whitney replied. He was here to see his family, except that he had come upon her first, and thankfully he didn't know a thing about what was going on. She hoped he would never know just how badly she had been subjugated.

"Where is my son? Council meeting?"

"Yes, I think so," Whitney replied, glancing quickly at the handsome profile beside her. Stewart's voice held paternal pride. Obviously he was happy to see Eagle fit so precisely into both worlds.

"Well, then," he said with a wink, "you and I will certainly get at him when he returns!"

"No . . . uh . . . please," Whitney protested, straining to wink in return. "I'll get him myself, if you don't mind. In fact, I'd appreciate it very much if you didn't mention that we've met. I have to . . . umm . . . I have to try and find your daughter — " she fabricated quickly. "I promised to tour a bit of the encampment with her and Randy."

"Okay," Stewart agreed mischievously. "I won't say a thing. But when you do find Katie and Randy, see if you can think of a good excuse to send them by here. I'll be in Naples for the next three weeks, but I'd like to surprise them all today."

"I'm sure they'll be surprised," Whitney said sweetly.

Impulsively she kissed Stewart's well-lined but attractive, endearing face. She could have grown very fond of him. So many subtle nuances of his had been inherited by his son! And she was in love with the son. . . . *No!* Whitney screamed to herself. No more. She would forget him, forget the nights when he had taught her the secrets of her own desires, forget the intensity of the intimacy they had shared.

No, she could never forget. But she could use the memory of his betrayal to strengthen her cause. He would be the fool this time.

"Mr. Stewart," she said, rising, "it has been a great pleasure, I assure you. I'm going to run now, if you don't mind. Morning Dew — I think — went visiting.

She should be back any minute. I do want to find Katie, if you'll excuse me."

"Surely!" Stewart rose next to her and accepted her offered hand. "And I promise you, my dear, the pleasure has been mine. I don't mind saying that I can see why my son kidnapped you! I look forward to our meeting again."

"Yes . . . yes. . . ." Whitney lied. She rushed away before he could see the trace of tears blurring her eyes. She blinked them away furiously. She had to think and move quickly. To make her getaway she would need to have complete control over her emotions!

Whitney forced herself to walk into the chickee she had shared with Eagle. Refusing to dwell upon any memories, she kept her gaze from the bedding, from the neat bundles of Eagle's clothing. It was good, she decided grimly, that he had made her travel light. Casting aside her Indian clothing, she scrambled into jeans and a blouse, looped the strap of her bag over her shoulder and hopped from the platform of her "honeymoon" suite once more — for the last time. With her eyes straight ahead, she resolutely walked the return trip on the trail. She couldn't look back. Her lips were already trembling.

Nearing the clearing, Whitney froze. The joyful sound of two distinct male voices came her way. Eagle had discovered that his father was there.

Unable to resist, Whitney crept wraithlike into the trees. The two men were embracing naturally — a father and son who not only loved but respected one another, both tall, strong and determined.

Whitney drew a jagged breath. Her eyes now were only for the son. She stared at him, as if by doing so she could etch every line and angle of him into her memory forever — the flashing blue eyes, the arrogant hawklike nose, the height of his proud cheekbones, the bronze of his smooth skin, the large, long-fingered, slightly calloused hands. . . . She closed her eyes, and still she saw him. Soon, though, she told herself, stiffening, he would know that his father had given him away. When she didn't reappear by nightfall, someone would grow worried. Then Stewart would have to admit that he had seen her.

And how would Eagle take the news? She was sure he would harbor no anger against his father. He would probably shrug and accept the fact that his game had been up a little early. He might even vaguely regret the loss of his bed partner. Then his blue eyes would begin to twinkle and he would anticipate their meeting — a meeting when he could look into her eyes with the amused knowledge that he had completely fooled and debased the imperious "Miss Virginia" who had wandered into his web.

Whitney strangled back a moan of anguish. How could she ever walk into his office? All the things he knew about her! Her past . . . her vulnerabilities! How could she ever look him in the eyes again? She couldn't.

She could turn around and leave the southern marshlands altogether. Take her BMW and head right back to marvelously cultured Virginia, where . . .

Her father and Gerry waited, expecting that she would find defeat on her own.

No. She would be dead and buried first. She had a few days left to lick her wounds and plan her strategy. Then she would face Mr. Jonathan Eagle Stewart on territory where she was familiar and practiced. And she would emerge the victor.

Whitney opened her eyes. With a final impression of blue-black hair, she shifted quietly through the foliage. Out of range of the Eagle clan sector, she began to run, desperation moving her quickly from the alligator pits to the council platforms to the nightly bonfire area. Where were they? Finally Whitney saw a patch of sandy hair in the midst of coal black. Randy was playing in a ball game. Katie had to be nearby.

Crunching her lip in preparation for the lie she was about to embellish, Whitney raced around the edges until she found Katie.

"Katie!" Whitney wailed desperately, startling the beautiful woman as she pounced upon her and swung her around. "Oh, Katie, I've been looking for you everywhere! I need help desperately. I — I have to get back to my car and I can't find Eagle."

"Calm down!" Katie soothed kindly, making Whitney wince. "Whatever it is, Randy and I will help you."

"You're going to think this terribly foolish of me," Whitney continued, hating herself but seeing no other way. "I forgot a rather serious problem. I have to be in Naples by evening. My father might be there, and if he doesn't find me he'll have the damned National Guard searching the Everglades. I am so sorry — " She *was* sorry to be inventing such an absurd tale. "It had all simply slipped my mind, but you don't know the man!"

Katie chuckled. "I know all about fathers. Mine kept me on a leash until I married Randy. Between him and Eagle, it's amazing we ever had a date!"

Whitney breathed a sigh of sick relief as Katie gestured to Randy to bring him to the sidelines. Katie explained the situation to her husband quickly, and if Randy thought such sudden panic wearisome, he gave no indication. "We'll get you out of here," he promised quickly.

"I hate to be such a bother," Whitney said sincerely.

"No bother. The trip to the car will only be an hour. An hour back . . ." Randy shrugged. "We won't miss anything. If you'd rather, though, I'm sure that I can find Eagle for you — "

"No! Um . . . I think he's with the council. If you're sure you don't mind, you can explain for me. I'll see him as soon as I can."

"Whatever you say," Randy agreed. He was wearing one of those concealed grins that clearly stated that compliance was much easier than trying to reason with a panicky woman, no matter how feeble her explanations. "If you're ready, we'll go. The airboat is tethered thataway."

Whitney turned her back on the Miccosukees and the Green Corn Dance. She was sorry to use Katie and Randy, but then it was fitting that Eagle's own sister and brother-in-law would be the instruments of her escape.

CHAPTER SEVEN

Alligator Alley was desolate even with a bright sun shining overhead. Whitney looked nervously at her gas-tank gauge, praying that her car would live up to its promised highway mileage and bring her the thirty remaining miles to a service station. She had no intention of ever making a trek into unknown swampland again.

It was amazing, Whitney thought, that she was driving normally. Her eyes were on the road, her hands on the wheel. She looked normal! Inside she felt like the fuming, bubbling lava of a volcano. If only she could erupt!

To ease her frustration she fiddled with the radio, trying to find a station. After a fair amount of static she landed on something clear. Unfortunately what she heard was a John Denver song. Just what she needed. Another reminder that the Miccosukee

187

Indians were well aware of the white world. Another reminder that Eagle had led her down a yellow brick road of fantasy, encouraging her belief that she dealt with backwoods people. . . .

She switched off the radio. Too bad she couldn't turn off her tormented mind with equal ease. None of it would have been so bad if only she hadn't fallen in love with him! *That,* she admitted in her deepest subconscious, was the root of her fury. And she had been dreaming that he loved her too and that at the end of the week some magical miracle would occur to keep them together.

And while she was dreaming, he was playing with her.

Whitney reached the service station and had her tank filled with gas and her car checked completely. The attendant gave her directions, and within another half-hour she was pulling into a motel in North Naples. Upon reaching her room she paced energetically back and forth. If nothing else, the vigorous exercise did drain some of the tension from her muscles.

"Civilization!" she proclaimed aloud. "Blessed civilization!" A thorough scrub in a scalding hot shower was at hand, then a quiet dinner and a glass of wine from room service.

No, a carafe of wine. She would drink the entire thing herself and then sleep until she woke. Sleep until her heartache eased. . . .

And it would ease, she promised herself stoically. Time was the healer. Tomorrow she would laze around the pool and check into the offices of T and C. By nightfall she would be ready to check out whatever nightlife Naples offered.

As if determined to erase the very essence of the past days, Whitney pampered herself ridiculously. She plucked her brows, shaved her legs, poured more than ample lotion into the bath water and smeared herself with perfumed skin conditioners she never used. She rolled her hair in electric curlers with a bitter grimace, and manicured her cracked nails.

Still, the trace of calluses remained on her hands. Just as the image of Eagle remained on her mind, within her, constant.

And even a full bottle of Sauvignon failed to put her to sleep with the comfort and ease of just knowing that Eagle was beside her.

After a brisk swim in the morning and an hour of soaking in the sun, Whitney called the offices of T and C, informing the secretary that she would be in after lunch to go over the briefings. The relief evident in the young woman's voice at hearing that Whitney had safely arrived sent little chills into her even before she heard the reason.

Whitney had always hated to lie, not simply because of principle but because of a faint tinge of superstition. Even for a necessary little fib, she would never use the excuse of someone being sick in case she should be foretelling the truth and that person become ill. She would never invent an accident.

And now she knew why. Her lie to Katie and Randy was coming true. Her father had been trying to contact her for the entire five days, and according to the secretary, he was beginning to sound like a madman. By tomorrow he would have helicopters searching the Glades and have an all-points alarm out.

"Damn!" Whitney groaned into the phone.

"I'm sorry, Miss Latham," Susie, the secretary apologized. "We've tried to assure him that you weren't late, that you probably were seeing a bit of the countryside. But he just wouldn't listen."

"Whitney," Whitney interposed automatically. "And please don't apologize. I do know my father! I'm sorry he has been harassing you! I'll get hold of him right away."

Whitney rang off quickly and stared rebelliously at the phone. "Damn!" she repeated inanely. When would he ever believe that she had grown up? It was embarrassing! Men were despicable creatures all the way around, she decided.

She picked up the phone and put her call through to Richmond. As soon as her father heard her voice, he expounded a lecture that sent Whitney hurling back to a pillow, holding the receiver away from her ear so that she wouldn't have to hear his words but would know when she was supposed to mutter a response.

"Dad!" she interjected once. "I'm a full quarter of a century old! I'm legal, remember, and adult! I never promised to call in!"

"You had your mother, Gerry and me worried silly!"

"Gerry and I are divorced."

"Another silly whim of yours."

Whitney exhaled and counted slowly. "Dad, I'm fine. I wanted to see a little of the terrain."

"Alone?"

She could almost see the veins bulging in her father's temple.

"No . . . uh . . . I had an Indian guide."

That was good for another five minutes on trusting no-account woodsmen.

"Dad," Whitney interrupted, wishing she

could simply record the word. "I was visiting a tribe of Miccosukee Indians. They are moral and upright people. I will be dealing with them — "Whitney broke off suddenly. She was furious with her father, she realized, and not because of the interference she had learned to tolerate from him. He was saying things wildly, in ignorance. *As she once had.* And she was left to defend the Indians.

Choosing her words carefully, Whitney went into her own lecture, telling her father in concise terms that the Indians were far more civil and trustworthy than most men she knew. Relenting at the end, she added softly, "I love you, Dad, and I wouldn't purposely hurt Mom for the world! But I'm a big girl. I can take care of myself."

"Hmmmph!" The phone was silent for a few seconds, then her father found a new vein of rebuke.

"And what is this 'Miss' they call you at the office? You are a 'Mrs.' "

"Actually, I'm a 'Ms.,' " Whitney said and started chuckling. "What on earth difference does it make?"

"You had a husband!"

"I don't now." Or did she? A strong, noble man with blue eyes. . . .

" — will be down late next week . . ."

"What?" Oh, God, what had he said while

she was wandering?

"Gerry. I'm sending him down. He needs a little sun and sand anyway, and you know how concerned he is, even if you did walk out on him."

"No, Dad, no."

"You mean you'd refuse to see him — as an old friend?"

"Of course not. It's just — "

"Good. You'll see him next week. He can accurately assess the situation. Take care of yourself, now, daughter, and we'll expect to hear from you soon."

The phone went dead. Whitney stared at it incredulously for countless seconds before she again turned to her pillow. Thank God none of them could see her now! she thought grimly, pounding her fist into the padded receptacle. They would label her certifiably insane and have her put away for good!

But she had to pound the pillow. When she was through, she would prepare to prove her strength of will calmly and ruthlessly to all of them, mindless of any toes that had to be stepped on.

The land problem proved to be far more complex than Eagle had explained. The Miccosukees and the Cow Creek Seminoles were two entirely different tribes, with separate interests. Both were claiming pieces of the land purchased from the government by T and C. Jonathan E. Stewart was representing both tribes, but separate deals had to be made with each.

Greg Tanner, the friendly, fortyish manager of the Naples office, scratched his forehead distractedly as he tried to explain the confusing situation. "Neither tribe is fiercely against selling land — it's this particular *piece* of land. Maybe a stubborn streak; I don't know. That's where you fit in. When you meet with Stewart, you'll hopefully understand."

Whitney smiled enigmatically. "I'm sure Mr. Stewart and I will understand one another perfectly," she purred.

"We do want that land," Greg said with a sigh.

"We'll get it," Whitney assured him. "The right amount of pressure might be just what Stewart needs. I think I know the pressure points."

"Oh, Whitney — " Susie stuck her head into the inner office and pushed her stylish gold-rimmed spectacles back up the bridge of her nose. "Mr. Stewart's secretary just called. She wanted to make sure the meeting was still on for today."

"Yes, it's still on," Whitney said and smiled. So Eagle thought he had sent her running!

"Mr. Stewart would like to make it lunch, then. One o'clock at the Golden Dragon. Will that be all right?"

"One thirty," Whitney corrected, "will be fine." She might as well let him have fair warning that he wouldn't be twisting her by the tail anymore!

Besides, she wanted to run back to her motel room before she met him. She wanted to be absolutely perfect — Miss Virginia to a *t*.

And she was. Her few days of lounging in the sun had given her a lovely golden tan, which she emphasized by wearing a cool white knit dress that left her arms and shoulders bare and lightly formed to her figure, flattering it in a subtle way that left the observer wondering how such a chaste dress could mold so accurately around slender curves. She left the feathery waves of her hair fluttering around her face while she swept the waist-length back portion into a sophisticated twirl that would add a few inches to her height. Her compact purse and trim heels were a matching green, coordinates to her eyes.

At precisely one thirty she arrived at the

Golden Dragon, sure that she would meet Eagle with cool, unflinching eyes.

Unfortunately she hadn't counted on Eagle's drastic change of appearance. She met him in the lounge, and she didn't flinch because she was too busy — to her extreme annoyance — gaping.

The long black hair was gone. It still reached to his collar, but the cut was stylish. He wore a vested navy pinstripe suit with a casual finesse that would immediately draw any feminine eye. The stark white of his tailored shirt set off a light blue tie to perfection — the silk was an exact match to his eyes. When his eyes finally lit upon her, Whitney momentarily forgot all her resolves. He had never looked sexier; he was refined, yet still rugged. Like a chameleon, he had changed to suit his environment and done it remarkably well. His Indian blood was still apparent; it always would be in the strong lines of his bronze face, but no one on earth would ever take him for an unsophisticated backwoodsman or question his capabilities in speaking the Queen's own English.

"Miss Latham." He stated her name coolly, with his blue gaze flicking lightly over her as he left his stance by the bar to greet her. A crooked smile came to his lips — the almost-sneer she had been expecting.

"What's the matter, cat got your tongue? I'm sure you have a lot to say."

"Of course I do!" Whitney snapped irritably. "I — it just took me a minute to recognize you."

"Really?" His brows rose in an arch of doubt, then he snapped his fingers and frowned in self-reproach. "I'm sorry! I forgot to wear my feathers! That would have led you right to me!"

"Droll!" Whitney retorted. "Very droll!" She could feel her temper rising and she was determined to remain cool and aloof.

Eagle placed a firm grip upon her elbow and led her from the lounge to the main dining room. "I guess we'd better take our places in the combat zone," he murmured as he walked, then smiled suavely to the maître d', who rushed to them with a deference that further annoyed Whitney. Her companion, it seemed, had the ability to make people jump wherever he went.

"Ah . . . Mr. Stewart! Right this way, sir. I have you and the lady set in the alcove," the white-jacketed man gushed. "Please don't hesitate to request anything at all. . . ."

Eagle himself seated a very stiff Whitney and nodded a friendly concordance. "Thanks, Henry. I'm sure things will be superb as usual."

Whitney immediately began to study the menu, although she wasn't really seeing a word. She needed time — time to adjust to the assault on her senses his mere presence instigated. During sleepless nights she had imagined his woodsy, masculine scent on the air . . . in her dreams his firm hands had caressed her skin . . . and now here he was, in the flesh, alive and vital. She had prepared herself; yet she now had to remind herself that she hated him. He had purposely made a complete idiot out of her. Time to bite back.

Outwardly Whitney exuded the aura she desired. Her appearance was that of a sophisticated, lovely young woman — confident, self-assured. A flick of an eyelash could convey disdain; a tilt of her head could draw instant response to a commanding authority.

Witch! Eagle thought bitterly, scanning her over the top of his own menu. She had her stubborn mind set. She had no intention of listening to anything he had to say. And it was all so stupid! He had the wild urge to drag her out of the restaurant and force her to listen to him, to force her back into his arms. The pain was like a hot coiled thing that gnawed away at him deep within.

He stiffened imperceptibly. Damn her beautiful little face straight to hell! She thought she had him now. Well, she didn't. She wanted a fight — a civil fight — and she was going to get one.

Suddenly she looked at him very sweetly. "I'm surprised you chose this place. I don't see catfish, alligator or *sofki* under the entrées."

"I'll suffer," Eagle returned. He politely took the silver lighter from Whitney's hand and lit the cigarette she had pulled from her bag. "May I suggest a bottle of their Sauvignon '72?"

"You may suggest anything you please."

Eagle would have liked to suggest a good swat on the rear end. Instead he returned her steady smile and met the hostile challenge in her eyes.

"The duckling a l'orange is excellent."

"Really?"

"Ah! And they do serve frog legs. I don't believe you've attempted that delicacy yet."

"There are certain things I have no desire to try, Mr. Stewart."

"And others you sample lavishly before suddenly deciding you have no taste for them?"

Whitney snapped her menu closed with precision and folded her hands over the snowy tablecloth. "One can find that certain things which are at first palatable leave an incredibly bitter aftertaste."

Eagle lightly lifted a brow and shrugged, but Whitney knew her barb had struck from the tic that pulsed in the hard line of his jaw. Smiling pleasantly through locked teeth, he reached nonchalantly across the table and casually lifted her right hand. Whitney tensed automatically, but trying to withdraw her hand from his hold, she discovered that his apparently light touch had the force of steel.

Smiling more deeply at her attempted resistance — and the dilemma that was obvious in her eyes with the realization that she must endure his touch or create an embarrassing scene — Eagle turned her palm upward and rubbed the soft flesh in a circular pattern with his thumb. He stared at her hand with mock admiration, then met her eyes again, drawling, "What lovely skin, Miss Latham. It's as silky as satin. Such exquisite perfection, to be marred by such a calloused tongue."

Whitney didn't need to jerk her hand away. He dropped it like a hot rock.

"If my tongue is calloused, Mr. Stewart, it has only become so recently, from what I believe is referred to as association with one afflicted with the forked-tongue syndrome." Whitney curtly delivered her speech without batting an eyelash.

The timely arrival of a stoic waiter saved Whitney from an immediate reprisal on her comment.

"I believe the lady wishes to order for herself," Eagle said coolly, inclining his head.

Whitney decided on the shrimp cocktail and roast lamb. Eagle ordered oysters on the half shell and frog legs. As an afterthought he ordered the wine. "Two glasses, please, although I'm not sure the lady will be joining me."

He stared at Whitney, his blue eyes glacial daggers, until the waiter returned with the wine and hovered uncertainly after Eagle's initial taste and murmur of, "Very good," perplexed over how to handle the situation.

"Miss Latham," Eagle prompted, "you have this poor man in distress. Wine?"

Whitney shrugged. "If you insist."

"Oh, Miss Latham," Eagle protested sardonically, "I never insist. But you know that."

Resisting an urge to kick him beneath the table, Whitney turned a dazzling smile on the waiter. "Thank you. I'll be delighted to try the wine."

The waiter poured the wine and promptly disappeared. Eagle raised his glass to her in a toast. "To 'civil' compromises."

Whitney raised her glass in return, quirking her lips with skepticism. "Certainly."

Eagle watched her as they sipped the wine. "I hope this is palatable, Miss Latham, and that you're not plagued by a bitter aftertaste."

"I doubt that I shall be, Mr. Stewart. This is a reputable establishment. I'm sure the wine lives up to its fine label."

"I see. What you see is what you get?"

"Precisely."

"You are reading books by their covers," Eagle mused with a twist of acid mirth. "Tell me, what difference does a change of jacket make — especially when you are well aware of the contents of the pages?"

His insinuations were brash, but Whitney, though fighting the color that threatened to engulf her, was determined not to let him wedge beneath her skin. She issued an exaggerated sigh and spoke to the rim of her wineglass. "Are we speaking of contents? Or another cliché? It seems you can take the man out of the swamp but not the swamp out of the man." Her gaze lifted pointedly to his. "I suppose I'm lucky you wore a shirt of any kind."

Calculated to demoralize, her comment brought a laugh instead. Mocking hurt shock, Eagle objected politely. "Miss

Latham! You wound me to the quick. I always wear a shirt. Except when I'm alligator wrestling. Or" — the timbre of his voice lowered a shade and his fingers lightly covered hers again — "when I'm bathing. Or in bed — sleeping, or engaging in other activities. But then I'm telling you things you already know again."

Whitney didn't need to worry about color. The blood drained from her face. She wrenched her fingers away quickly so that he couldn't sense their trembling and curled them around her wineglass. She couldn't chance meeting his eyes and stared at the golden liquid instead. The gentle caress of his fingertips alone had filled her mind with startling recall, heating a core deep within her — a traitorous physical core. But she had to indifferently deny him. . . .

"My memory can be short, Mr. Stewart, very short. Especially when things are best forgotten. We are here to discuss land, anyway, not clothing."

"You brought up the subject, Miss Latham, not I."

"Fine, then I shall also drop it."

Neither one of them had raised his or her voice a hair, nor had they dropped the glacial smiles that twisted their faces into frozen masks of conviviality. Still, the -

atmosphere itself was charged. Whitney realized just how thick an aura of animosity surrounded them when the waiter chose to return at that moment. He served their appetizers with trembling fingers and dashed away, practically tripping over the wine stand.

"Let's get to land, Mr. Stewart," Whitney said, glad she could concentrate on spearing her shrimp. "I'll be very blunt. We're prepared to offer the Indians — both tribes — substantial restitution. If you don't care to accept our generous offers, I shall be more than happy to drag you into court."

Eagle calmly swallowed an oyster. "May I say, Miss Latham, that I'm glad you are with the diplomatic corps of T and C Development and not the United Nations?"

Whitney smiled and viciously twisted her lemon wedge. "As I've told you, Mr. Stewart, you may say or suggest anything you please."

"A charming concession," Eagle grated.

"Well?"

"You will not get that land, Whitney."

"But I will — Mr. Jonathan 'White Eagle' Stewart."

Eagle dipped his head and swallowed his last oyster, and the appetizer plates were immediately whisked away. Their entrées were carefully served and more wine poured — by the maître d', Whitney noticed vaguely, rather than their nerve-racked waiter.

"How is the lamb, Miss Latham?" Eagle inquired politely.

"Quite tender, thank you."

Cutting a morsel of his own food, Eagle chewed thoughtfully. "Tender and delectable," he mused. "However, I — like you — have recently discovered how the most tender and delectable . . . ah . . . tastes . . . can become quite sour. One is enticed to feast and then *voilà!* The banquet disappears!"

Banquet! He had made his statement innocently, innocuously, but still his voice rang with caustic insinuation. She had never been anything more than a diversion, like a meal, pleasingly gourmet as it may have been. Her face was no longer ashen; it flooded scarlet. The man had no scruples whatsoever. Neither would she. Her temper was rising, but she had to keep cool. They were on her territory now, and a verbal battle was one she could win.

"Banquet, sir? Rather a fish hooked and dangled on a line, deceived by the lie of a lure. But even fish that look like easy prey can sense deception and slip hooks."

"I see. Now we're talking about wolves in sheep's clothing."

"You flatter yourself, Stewart," Whitney flared. "We're talking about liars, con men, despicable cheats — " she choked off her own words. What was she saying, she wondered sinkingly. He was goading her into comments that were childishly imperious. Even while wishing she could take back her remark, she knew she couldn't. Her name-calling was below the belt, but she couldn't afford the weakness of an apology. Whatever he thought of her snobbishness, he would just have to think.

Eagle's eyes narrowed to slits of ice blue. "You intend to make two tribes of Indians suffer because you imagine you've been done a wrong by one man?"

Whitney pushed at her lamb toyingly with her fork. She had lost her appetite. "Suffer? I don't intend to make anyone suffer. You took me out to meet the Indians so that I could have a good understanding of what I was doing. Well, I do. I'm convinced that they need all the help I can give them. Grinding corn all day may be your idea of amusement, but it isn't mine. There is no need for anyone to spend every waking moment in grueling labor these days. There is no need for anyone to live in a thatched hut. The community we're offering will provide well-paying jobs for men and women alike.

Surely you can't resent that, Mr. Stewart."

"I don't resent your community. Build it, by all means. The economic advantages will most certainly be enjoyed by some; the interaction between the white and Indian societies will no doubt be beneficial. I'm simply afraid that you'll have to build elsewhere. I will be happy to help you find another suitable spot."

"Mr. Stewart, we had men in the field for months trying to find the perfect location," Whitney said stubbornly, positive that she held the edge. That Eagle had pushed aside his own plate and now stared at her calmly, his arms crossed confidently over his chest as he leaned back in his chair, merely served to strengthen her determination.

"The land is not perfect if it belongs to someone else."

Whitney expelled a condescending sigh of exasperation. "We are willing to buy the land for more than it is actually worth! Honestly, *White Eagle,* there are times when I feel they definitely misnamed you! Balking Mule would have been much more apt!"

"How clever!" Eagle arched a black brow high. "Coffee, Miss Latham?" Without her consent, he motioned to the waiter, who set steaming cups before them. When they were again alone, he moved like a coiled snake and leaned across the table. His voice was a smooth, silky hiss that left Whitney struggling with her willpower simply not to jump back from his advance.

"Since we're being clever here, Whitney, I'll let you in on an astute observation. Someone should take you over a knee, plant a few good whacks on your behind and send you back to Virginia to be grounded until you grow up! I'm sure you have brains and a mind, but I'm equally sure that you must be sitting on them! You won't be winning this one. If you persist in this cause — still not understanding a thing that's going on even though it all sits directly beneath your haughty little nose — you're likely to propel yourself right out of a job."

Blood spewed into Whitney's head and her temples began to pound furiously as she gasped in outrage. "How dare you!" she grated, unable to keep a cool tone in her voice any longer. "Of all the audacious, arrogant and egotistical statements! I can guarantee you that I will not be out of a job! It is you, Mr. Stewart, who will find yourself on the defensive! *You* who will lose — a fool through and through to both communities by the time I finish with you! You may have an advantage in the backwoods of the Everglades, Eagle, and you certainly did manage a few tricks! But we are far from there now. Nor can you keep me from discovering real truths!" Gritting her teeth, Whitney spoke her last words between them, very slowly. "I — will — bring — you — down!"

Eagle didn't quirk a muscle. The only sign of his own anger was a pulse that worked furiously in twin veins along the sides of his taut neck. Motioning again to the waiter, he silently signed the check. With silent menace he assisted Whitney from her chair and firmly escorted her from the restaurant. Wincing with protest at the iron grip propelling her, Whitney tried to wrench her arm away. "Stop it!" Eagle hissed in her ear. "This is one of your 'civilized' restaurants, and I refuse to brawl in public!"

A moment later they were standing in the parking lot by the BMW. "Give me your keys!" Eagle growled.

"I hardly think — "

"You're right. You don't think. Give me the damn keys." Eagle curtly grasped them from her fumbling fingers and none too politely ushered her into the car. "Don't worry," he advised acidly as he joined her, "I won't be with you long. I only have one or two things to say, but you are going to listen to them without a pack of snotty remarks in return."

"I don't have to — "

"The hell you don't!" Eagle's grip was now around her wrist, and she could barely twist her fingers, much less escape him. His handsome face, tense and rigid with anger, was inches from her own. A quivering of fear began to dance over her spine and she stared motionlessly into the flaring, hypnotizing blue of his eyes.

"Now, Miss Latham, since I seem to have your attention, I shall try to be very diplomatic. The land you have chosen has special tribal value to the Indians. Sentiment — not dollars and cents. No matter what you offer, they will not sell. And they can prove in a court of law that the land is theirs. Keep your vendetta against me personal and wise up about the land. You'll hurt a lot of people by trying to spite me."

"I'm not making a business decision out of spite!" Whitney sputtered. "I know they can use what I want to give them!"

"Then handle this with the PR with which you are supposedly so proficient!"

"I — "

"Shut up for a minute!" Eagle commanded harshly. "Take some time and think. What you are doing is because of me, and I'm not even sure quite why. Just exactly what did I do to you? I couldn't tell you who

I was that night — you would have put on your little professional act immediately, and I wouldn't have been able to make you understand a thing. I never lied to you. I am White Eagle and I did bring you to my family and they do live that way! Yes, some of our people have electricity and modern conveniences and some even live in your whitewashed houses! It's your anger against me that is keeping you from seeing anything! I gave you a culture, Whitney, and it doesn't seem to mean a damned thing to you! All you see is dollar signs and grocery stores and washing machines."

"You gave me a culture!" Whitney blurted furiously. "You did a hell of a lot more than that. You — you — "

"I what? I made love to you? I let you know that you were very much alive? That you were a warm, sensuous woman? You want to destroy me because of that?"

"Don't be ridiculous!" Whitney seethed. "You keep flattering yourself. You're not so incredibly special! I — I loathe your touch, I — "

"You," Eagle interrupted scathingly, encircling her other wrist, "have turned into more than a self-righteous, misinformed do-gooder. You've become a liar."

"A liar!" Her voice was rising to a shrill

shriek. "Get out of my car!"

"I intend to — in just a minute." He had twisted over her now, and his breath was a warm, moist breeze against her cheeks. "I'm giving you fair warning, Whitney. I can take you, and if you force my hand, I will. I can take you in any game you want to play."

"You'll have to prove that!" she hissed.

"I will."

The lips that had been hovering over hers were suddenly upon them, bruising and demanding. The assault was so swift that Whitney was momentarily in shock, unable to protest. By the time she gathered her wits back together, he had taken total advantage of the situation, prying into the cavern of her mouth with an insistent tongue. And in her stupor she was responding. Her senses had taken over, and after the days of deprivation, there was nothing more natural than the sweet, addictive ambrosia of his masculine lips invading hers, or the delicious eroticism of his commanding hands seeking the swells of her breasts, which rose automatically to curve for his pleasure as she arched to him. . . .

"*No!*" Logic, reason and fury finally tamed the wanton, instinctive physical response. Pushing the slender fingers that had risen to entangle in his black hair against him, Whitney echoed the choked scream. Eagle acquiesced — at his own speed, releasing her slowly. Whitney met the sardonic amusement in his eyes with desperate venom. She was dangerously close to tears she would never allow him to see her shed.

"Get out of my car — now!"

"I'm going." He sounded infuriatingly unperturbed, as well he should. He had controlled the kiss from the beginning. Had he chosen, Whitney thought with horror, he could have easily overridden her feeble objection. "I think," he said concisely, exiting the BMW with his fluid motion, "that I have proved my point."

Whitney watched in stunned immobility as he walked across the parking lot, tall, sinewed and exceedingly masculine in the perfectly tailored jacket that accentuated the breadth of his shoulders and the trimness of his hips and long legs. Then a white-hot flash of heat invaded her with renewed fury. She stormed from the BMW after him, catching up with him just as he entered the driver's seat of his own car, a quiet gray Mercedes.

Clutching the windowsill with white-knuckled hands, Whitney rushed into scathing speech. "You haven't proved a thing, Mr. Stewart," she declared vehemently. "You play tricks and take people un-aware. That is all. I happen to know that I am right. That land is right where it should be — accessible! To your people. I intend to show them the benefits, and I intend to bring you into a court of law, where your devious ways will be ripped to shreds. I, Mr. Stewart, am giving you fair warning. Take some time yourself and go out and find yourself a good lawyer!"

A deadly grin stretched Eagle's grim lips.

"My dear Miss Latham, I am a lawyer. You just don't ever seem to have the pertinent facts, do you? I'm even considered to be a good lawyer. That's why I — an outsider — am representing the Indians."

The volcano was about to spew forth. Whitney spun on her heels just as the Mercedes roared into action.

CHAPTER EIGHT

It was a terrible thing to suspect you might be wrong, Whitney thought as she shifted in her lawn chair before the pool and tossed her towel over her burning face. Terrible, when you wanted so desperately to be right!

Almost a week had passed since her luncheon encounter with Eagle. Hate and anger had sustained her through the first few days; then uncertainty had set in. Was she so bent on vengeance that she had become blind? T and C had supported her ultimatum that they take the matter to court, but now she was doubting her own single-minded vision. A woman scorned, she thought bitterly. Well, her tantrums with Eagle could hardly be called mature.

"Aha! I've found you! Believe it or not, old man that I am, I would recognize that body anywhere!"

Whitney ripped the towel from her face

and stared incredulously at the crinkling blue eyes of a smiling Jonathan L. Stewart. He was clad today in tan leisure slacks and a beige tennis shirt, and as he stood above her, his hands idly in his pockets, Whitney was again struck by the resemblance between father and son. Unwittingly she smiled. There was little else to do when met with the dazzling, genteel gaze of the senior Stewart.

"I hear you're on the outs with my son," Stewart said cheerfully, drawing another lawn chair next to Whitney's. "I hope you won't hold that against the father."

Whitney grinned sheepishly. "No, sir."

"Call me Jon," he suggested. "All my friends do."

"No, Jon," Whitney said. "I hold nothing against you." She frowned and grimaced suddenly and reached for her dark sunglasses in a pretense of blinking from the heat of the sun. He must know everything now! she thought in a rash of embarrassment. Well, not *everything*, but enough to allow his imagination to do the rest.

"Did your son send you here?" she asked suspiciously.

Jon chuckled. "You must be kidding, Miss Latham. My son is as stubborn — if not more so — as you are. I think he would stand his ground until the next Ice Age overtook it."

"Oh." She didn't voice the question, but it was in the air: *Then why are you here?*

"I'd like to see if you'd be willing to humor a senior citizen and spend an afternoon with me. I'll promise the reward of an excellent dinner in exchange for any boredom you have to endure," Jon said solemnly.

"Is this an appeal to my better nature?"

"Yes, frankly it is. If I know my son, if he became irritated, he never would get around to explaining things fully."

He didn't, Whitney thought silently. I didn't give him much of a chance.

"I shall be delighted to spend the afternoon with you, Jon."

"Good! Oh . . . uh . . . we won't mention this to anyone, if that's agreeable."

Whitney rose and stretched, chuckling. "*I* certainly won't say anything! Where are we going and what should I wear?"

Thirty minutes later they were back along a lonely stretch of Alligator Alley. A natural, comfortable friendship had grown between them, and they had discussed everything from world politics to the atrocious cost of meat in the supermarkets. Jon hadn't brought up his son's name. Neither had Whitney.

Jon's eyes slid from the road to Whitney.

"Know where we are yet?"

"If I'm not mistaken," Whitney replied, "from the maps I've seen, we're close to 'the' land."

"Precisely."

Whitney stared into the marsh. There wasn't a thing about the area of swampland that could remotely be termed special. As if reading her mind, Jon curled his lips. "You won't see anything," he told her. "Not until we park."

"Park?" Having been away from the crude environ of the Glades, Whitney shivered involuntarily.

"Trust me!" Jon said with a laugh, and Whitney smiled feebly. Hadn't the son said much the same thing?

They turned onto a path that remained hard and solid for several miles. Eventually it wound around to bring them to a small hammock.

"This is part of the land parcel," Stewart said amiably. With a friendly arm around her shoulder, he led Whitney down a pretty, overgrown trail of flower-strewn pines. A moment later he stopped.

At first Whitney didn't see anything unusual. That was because all the earth tones blended in the scenery. Then she realized that there was a box ahead in a small clearing, resting upon a squat structure of logs. Alongside the six-foot box were strewn tattered and half-buried remnants of pottery, utensils and fabric. Years of exposure to the elements had made the entire picture part of the landscape, but as Whitney swallowed a lump in her throat, she could slowly discern bits and pieces of a human life. From ashes to ashes; dust to dust. She didn't need to ask where she was.

"The land is a burial ground," she whispered weakly.

"Yes," Stewart said softly.

An eerie feeling of pain seemed to transmit itself from the elderly man to Whitney, and she was suddenly sure of something else. They hadn't just stumbled upon any grave.

"This is your wife's — Eagle's mother's — grave."

"Yes," Stewart said again simply. He made no move to go closer to the coffin but stood in silent meditation for a moment. Then he squeezed Whitney's shoulders and led her back along the trail. They were in the car again before either of them spoke.

"Are there others?" Whitney asked softly.

"Many," Jon Stewart replied. "The government has begun to offer interment in special plots, but the grave site you've just seen is the way of the Miccosukees. For countless years they have taken their dead into remote spots in the swamp. Civilization has been closing in, but the swamp is vast. My wife, as I believe Katie told you, was half white, yet she was raised as a Miccosukee. It was her wish to die as one."

"What was she like?"

The wistful question was out before Whitney realized she had voiced it. Stewart didn't seem to mind. A tender smile filtered onto his lips with beautiful poignancy.

"She was everything to me — the sun, the moon, the stars. Lovely, soft, gentle. She had a way with her . . . even wounded animals found their way to her doorstep, whether we were in the woodland or in my town house in the city. Katie is much like her mother."

"What — what happened?" Whitney asked thickly.

Jon shrugged. "A stray bullet from an out-of-season poacher."

"Oh, God!" Whitney's whisper was half gasp and half sob. "I'm really so very sorry."

Jon Stewart lifted a hand from the wheel to pat hers briefly. "Don't be, really; not for me. I was a very lucky man. Not everyone gets to find love like that."

He was quiet during the long drive back, and Whitney was left to her reflections. The man beside her, she decided, was extra-ordinary. He spoke of life and love with a grave simplicity that was astounding in its depth. Man enough openly to declare his emotions with romantic reverence, he had lived his beliefs regardless of obstacles or opinions. Whitney was sure he would never marry again, yet his lost love did not make him morose. It was something he treasured quietly in the recesses of his heart.

And suddenly, as she sat mutely in the car, Whitney knew exactly what she wanted in life. To love and be loved — like J. L. Stewart and his Indian bride. To find a love that sup-ported her and could sustain itself against the problems and idiosyncrasies of living together, a light in any darkness.

She sighed shakily. There was a man she could love that way. The man on whom she had declared bitter war.

"I promised you dinner," Jon said with a cheerful smile, "and I know a terrific little place on the shore, if you like seafood."

"Love it," Whitney assured him.

The restaurant did offer wonderful fresh seafood served in a rustic atmosphere that was pleasant and relaxing. Through the meal Whitney found herself confiding in Jon Stewart naturally, although she didn't go into much detail. She talked about her childhood, Virginia and even her brief marriage. Stewart, in return, talked about Chicago and his love for museums and theaters, and then how he loved to come back to Naples and spend quiet, peaceful times in the Glades with nature.

"I'm not much of a hunter," he told her, "but I do love to fish and I'm an avid bird-watcher!"

Their meeting at the Corn Dance was never brought up, nor was any mention of Eagle. The tone of their discussion had been so mellow and lulling that Whitney was taken by complete surprise when Stewart returned her to her motel room and bluntly asked, "What are you going to do now?"

"I — I suppose I'll battle T and C and look for other land," Whitney said. "I think I can eventually swing it."

"Will you tell my son?"

"No," Whitney said softly. "If we can come up with something else, he'll know when we meet in the planning conference."

Stewart hesitated for a second, then cleared his throat. "Whitney, I don't tend to interfere in other people's business, and I won't say much now. I know Eagle played quite a trick on you, but I think you might want to take a look at his motives."

Whitney bit her lip. She longed for the release of throwing herself into the gentle arms of the kindly, paternal man who had become her friend and to confess all that she was feeling, but she couldn't. She felt that she knew Eagle's motives all too clearly.

No, they had not been vicious. Devilish would be more like it. He had treated her to rare streaks of kindness and understanding. But to him it had all meant nothing. He had given, but in that giving he had torn her to shreds.

And she did still have her pride. The man had accomplished the feat easily of making an unmitigated fool of her.

"Jon," Whitney said lightly, "you have done your good deed for the day. I will get to work on a rational solution to this thing. But I have no intention of renewing a friendship with your son. And," she said as she grinned with rueful bitterness, "I sincerely doubt if your son cares one way or another. If he feels anything for me, I'm sure an accurate description might be contemptuous indifference." She felt herself beginning to blush. Should she add that Eagle might have found her an amusing bedmate? God forbid! This man she respected was most certainly well aware already of the more embarrassing details!

Damn! she thought, meeting his astute

blue gaze. He was reading her mind! "Whitney," he said gently, "I'm going to say one more thing and leave. I promise. I don't expect any response. But listen, and then think about what I say. I know my son. His greatest sin is pride. He would never come to you now. But he married you in a ceremony that he holds sacred. He loves you, and if I haven't gone senile I'm pretty sure you're in love with him too."

"He doesn't love me, Mr. Stewart," Whitney said with quiet dignity. "He married me because he loves his grandmother. He was very careful to tell me it wouldn't be a legal commitment. Besides . . ." she tried a nonchalant chuckle, "he married me when we had only known one another a few days. It's impossible to be in love that fast."

Stewart shrugged with an easy grin. "Oh, I don't know about that. I opened my eyes once and fell in love before I could blink. But I promised I wouldn't say anything more. I'm going to get going. And remember — our whole day is a secret, okay?"

"I'll remember," Whitney vowed.

She had barely closed the door before the phone started to ring.

"Whitney?"

The voice, she knew immediately, belonged to Katie. For an uncontrollable minute she started to laugh. It seemed that every Stewart she knew wanted to talk to her — except the one whose voice she wanted desperately to hear.

"Whitney? Are you there? Are you all right?"

"Yes, Katie," Whitney said, sobering. "I'm fine. What can I do for you?"

"I wanted to know if you were still interested in visiting the reservation and some of the independent villages along the Trail."

"Yes, I'd like very much to do some visiting," Whitney admitted. "When?"

"Tomorrow would be good for us — it's Sunday. How is that for you?"

"Fine."

They agreed on an early start, and just before she hung up, Katie asked the inevitable question.

"Oh — uh — Whitney, you won't mention this to my brother?"

"No, Katie, I won't," Whitney said dryly. "I really don't expect that I'll be talking to your brother."

There was nothing on the wire for several seconds except a slight static. "I'll — ah — see you in the morning, then," Katie said.

By late afternoon of the following day Whitney felt that she had been through a crash course on history and current events.

Her curiosity over the Miccosukees had become insatiable, and she knew it had little to do with her job. She had reentered Eagle's world, and all that she learned was as much a part of him as the stunning and immaculately tailored suit he had worn to their elegant luncheon. She couldn't have him, but somehow being with Katie among the Indians was strangely comforting — although it also brought memories that ripped her heart to anguished pieces.

During the day she met men and women who lived extremely varied lives. She visited homes that ranged from the typical chickee to the whitewashed house of her own community. Some of the Indians, like Morning Dew, stayed in the densest woods and lived off the land, while others held important jobs. She even learned how electricity could be installed in a chickee.

As the day drew to a close Whitney stood with Katie near the cattle pens on the reservation, watching the final roundup as she chewed on a blade of grass. As she crunched into the sweet root, a frown furrowed its way deeper and deeper into her brow.

"What is that look for?" Katie demanded with a chuckle.

Whitney glanced at her guiltily. They had skirted the subject of Eagle and the past all day, but now it was she who wanted to ask a question.

"I've been wondering . . . I mean, I don't understand your brother at all." Whitney glanced shamefaced at her hands to avoid Katie's eyes. "When I came down here I guess I really felt that the Indians needed help and that that was why they had a white man handling their affairs. Why didn't he start out by showing me how brilliant some of these men are — how far they have come in so many ways?"

Katie climbed up on the fence and stared out at the horizon, where the golden beauty of the setting sun in the Everglades could be seen. "You just said it yourself, Whitney. 'How far they have come.' Don't you see, you're going by your standards, which are fine. Our people are firm believers in live and let live. If you want a nine-to-five job in the city and a little yellow house with green trim and a flower garden, that's fine. But a lot of these people like to live in the Glades, the way their ancestors did for centuries. My grandmother grinds corn because she wants to. My father and brother are both wealthy men. Morning Dew could have anything in the world she wants. But she does have what she wants: custom and culture. She is happy to tend her garden and greet her family when they come back to her and the old ways, seeking comfort from the modern world. And we do go back to her, all of us. Eagle and I were raised to have pride in all that we are. I love my father and all that he is. And I love my grandmother, and I'm fiercely proud to be a Miccosukee. I can't speak for my brother, but I don't think he ever intended to hurt you. To tease you, yes; that's Eagle's way. He can be fierce, but I've never known my brother to be malicious. Have I made any sense?"

"Yes," Whitney said quickly. "Yes, of course." Ridiculous tears were forming in her eyes. Blinking rapidly, she pretended to feel a pebble in her boot and bent to remove it, shake it and put it back on.

"I think I should tell you, Katie," she said clearly, "that I'm going to try to find new land. I may have problems with the company, so I'm not going to make any promises. We could still wind up bitter opponents in a long drawn-out court battle."

Katie laughed and jumped off the fence. "I'm not worried. We have certain sayings among our people. One of them fits you well, and it's a particular favorite of my family. When someone goes after something with determination and integrity, we say that they fly like an eagle. You, Whitney, fly like an eagle."

"Thanks," Whitney said and grinned. "That's quite a compliment. But, then, I've been flying with a few Eagles, so I've had some practice!"

It was so easy to hug Katie. Why was it, Whitney wondered, that she could earn the love and respect of the entire family except for the son?

Convincing T and C that another spot could be found for the community was a long and tedious job, especially after she had originally sworn to see the thing through in court and fight it out. The hierarchy sympathetically understood the intricacies of invading a burial ground, but Whitney was sure that the chairman of the board would dig up his own mother for a profitable venture. It fell to her to find new land, solve the problems of land fill and access roads and even deal with the new complaints of the builders. All within a suffocating schedule.

But she did it. A plot of land owned neither by the Indians nor by the government as national park space was finally located. Things began to fall into place and finally meshed on the Friday morning just before the conference scheduled for T and C management and members of the Seminole and Miccosukee councils — and Jonathan E. Stewart.

As she sat waiting at the vast conference table in the pleasant but contemporary and austere meeting room, Whitney shuffled her papers and plans in a supreme effort to appear poised and unruffled.

She wasn't feeling in the least calm or sure of herself. She yearned for a sight of Eagle, but she desperately feared her reactions. Just knowing that he would walk through the door at any minute was causing her pulse to beat erratically at atrocious speed. Her palms remained moist no matter how many times she tried to dry them on a tissue. She was terrified that the pounding of her heart would muffle her speech.

That was one fear she needn't have worried about. When he walked up and stood in the doorway, nodding to her curtly before his cool blue gaze swept over the room, her heart seemed simply to stop. One glance at his broad shoulders, encased today in tan tweed, his stern, rugged profile and his tall, imposing figure was all she needed to stop her entire respiratory process. She couldn't look his way again. Draining the water glass before her to ease a throat that had turned to cotton, Whitney returned her sightless gaze to her papers. Soon the room was full — and as soon as she looked up, Whitney wished she could crawl under the conference table and disappear.

She had completely forgotten that the council would consist of the same men she had stood before for her Miccosukee wedding.

Whitney felt like a frozen mold. She vaguely heard all the company introductions; then she was being asked for the proposal. She managed to stand, then she managed to make her lips move. She was thankful that all her information was in front of her in black and white; if it hadn't been, she wouldn't have even remembered what they were talking about.

The conference, she saw vaguely, was her victory. The Indians, Seminole and Miccosukee alike, who were as capable as Eagle of remaining completely stoic and giving no hint of any emotion, actually smiled. T and C Development employees were looking equally pleased; it was advantageous to look like the nice guy.

Whitney was the only one in the room who felt ill. As soon as she finished her presentation, she whispered the excuse of a severe headache to her associates and slunk quietly from the room. She couldn't face either Jonathan Eagle Stewart or the Miccosukee council. The refuge of her motel room was all that she sought.

But driving into the motel's parking lot, Whitney became convinced that there was such a thing as karma — and that she had done something truly rotten in a previous life to deserve the day she was having. Something that decreed she receive full and drastic punishment.

For standing at her door, impatiently studying his wristwatch, was her ex-husband, Gerry Latham. Slim, impeccable, graying Gerry. Mr. Right. Her father had carried out his threat.

It was difficult to conceal her irritation as she slammed the door of the BMW, gathered her briefcase and handbag and clicked her heels across the concrete as she walked to meet him.

"Hello, Gerry."

"Thank goodness you got here," he began immediately, taking her things and her room key in complete charge and efficiency. "I've been worried sick! Isn't that job of yours finished at five o'clock? I thought you'd been dragged back into the woods by another Indian!"

"What?"

"Your father told me all about it." Gerry

looked distastefully around the adequate room and sighed. "You know, Whitney, I really don't understand you. We had such a beautiful home! A really nice thing. You are so young . . . I can see where you needed a little more time, but all this is so absurd — "

"Gerry, Gerry, wait." Whitney held up a hand and sank wearily into a recliner. "Stop. Whoa. Hold it. Let me correct you. I wasn't dragged into the woods by an Indian." A spark of mischief lit into her. "It was just the opposite. I dragged the Indian into the woods. And I molested him terribly!"

"Whitney!"

She should have had some sympathy for his look of horror, but after her long day she couldn't seem to help herself.

"Oh, Gerry! You just don't know! All those dances and secret meetings! It's so incredible — you couldn't imagine. The wild parties every night. . . ." He was still staring at her with such a dumbstruck expression that Whitney finally relented. "Gerry, I'm kidding. Believe me, dear ex, even you couldn't question the virtue of those Indians!"

Gerry shook his head and seated himself on the bed, musing over his slim hands. "I don't like it, Whitney. Neither does your father."

"Oh, Gerry! What's to like or dislike? This

is my life!" Whitney settled her forehead in her palm and sighed. "And anyway, I've been working for T and C for years now! It's a highly reputable company. I'm good at what I do, and I enjoy it." The satisfaction of all that she had achieved warmed her, along with an old affection for a friend. Gerry would never understand her, but he did care about her. "Come on," she told him, rising and patting the top of his head. "Let's go get some dinner and I'll tell you about my job."

Maybe it was a good thing that Gerry had shown up, Whitney decided as they sipped predinner cocktails. If he hadn't, she would probably have given in to the tide of emotions surging through her and spent the evening in a crying jag. Being with Gerry didn't take Eagle out of her mind; he was always in her mind; she was always waging battles against herself. Sometimes she dreamed that the phone would ring and it would be Eagle calling her. But he didn't call. It was becoming increasingly obvious that he cared nothing for her, and that if he ever had, she had doused his feelings with her irate behavior. Sitting alone in her room at night, she would fight herself when her heart demanded that she find him, beg his forgiveness and be anything to him, even a casual playmate. Then she would come to grips with herself. She wouldn't allow him to make an even greater fool of her. But the pain of seeing him today. . . .

"So where is the new land?"

"Pardon?"

"The land. Whitney, have you been paying any attention to me?"

"I'm sorry, Gerry. It's not far. I'll show you the new site tomorrow if you like."

"I might as well see what you're getting into," Gerry replied grimly. "Although why on earth you want to run around playing in some godforsaken swamp — "

"Gerry," Whitney interrupted impatiently, "I do not play. I work, and I've worked particularly hard to make this whole thing come about amicably . . ." Whitney's final words trailed into a convictionless whisper. Beyond Gerry's shoulder, she saw the arrival of a handsome couple at the bar. The woman was a tall, willowy, natural blonde, probably a few years older than herself.

The man was Eagle, strikingly debonair in black velvet.

Whitney was vaguely aware that Gerry had launched into another lecture, luckily one that required little response. Her eyes and mind were on the dark, raven-haired man who towered above his slim companion and solicitously escorted her to a bar stool.

His blue gaze was light, radiating a devastating masculine charm and charisma as he leaned to catch a response from the pale, lovely blonde.

Whitney had never known that jealousy could be such a brutal emotion. It washed over her in waves of agony, drying her throat, strangling her breath and seeming to stab a thousand little daggers into her insides. While Gerry droned on, she desperately tried to breathe normally and drag her riveted eyes from the couple before Eagle could see her.

Succeeding painfully in bringing her attention back to her escort, Whitney interrupted him. "Gerry, let's go. I — I'm getting a ghastly headache."

Gerry stopped speaking and peered at her suspiciously through the muted light of the lounge. "You do look pale — almost green in here! Swamp fever, I'll bet," he said with satisfaction. "You should have never — "

"Oh, for God's sake, Gerry! I do not have swamp fever!"

"Then you must need something to eat. We've already given our name for a table. We'll dine as soon as possible and leave."

Every bone in Whitney's body felt as if it had gone as stiff as steel. "Gerry, I do not want to eat. I am not a child, and I know what I want. You stay if you're hungry. I'm leaving."

But she didn't get a chance to leave. Even as she leaned across the small cocktail table to hiss her words with quiet vehemence, a feeling of acute unease was making her senses tingle. Before she could withdraw from the apparent intimacy of her position, she knew beyond a doubt that Eagle had seen her and had come to their table. The light scent that was enticingly pleasant yet all male was on the air, though his footsteps were as silent in the lounge as they were on the trails of the marsh.

"Good evening, Miss Latham. Sir — " Eagle nodded to Gerry with stiff courtesy. "I hope you'll excuse the interruption, but I'd like to have a word with you, Whitney. Perhaps your friend won't mind if I steal you for a dance. I promise to return you directly."

Eagle had no concern for a reply from either Gerry or Whitney. He coralled her elbow and assisted her up while still speaking, turned a daring smile to Gerry while his eyes caught his in a frosty chill, and led her out to the dance floor, where a few couples were already swaying to the easy tempo of a mellow country band.

Whitney was stunned and spellbound.

Still paralyzed by the jolt of his unexpected appearance, she was further bewitched and rattled by the inner tremors elicited by his manipulating touch. She had no thought for the blonde, or for Gerry, for that matter. Thought in its entirety had been swept aside momentarily by pure sensation.

And as they came together on the dance floor, Whitney experienced a rush of bliss. She nestled into his arms as if their forms had been made as a perfect fit for one another. Her head rested automatically on his shoulder; his chin was tickled by the soft silk of her hair. The arms that held her were fierce and possessive — angry, Whitney thought on a whim. Yet she would willingly take angry; she would take anything. . . .

"I wanted to thank you on behalf of the tribal councils, Miss Latham," Eagle said curtly, dispelling the cloud of dreams upon which Whitney waltzed with the glacial tone of his voice. "I'm glad that you decided to see reason. You saved us all quite a bit of trouble with an early surrender."

Surrender! Was that how he saw her endless hours of work? A cowardly surrender because of fear of a meeting with him in court?

It was impossible to pull out of his arms, but he surely must have felt the steel that meshed into her spine. "My 'surrender,' as you call it, Mr. Stewart, had nothing to do with you whatsoever! I simply came across a few people who considered me bright enough to comprehend the spoken word. They merely explained the situation to me, and with amazing clarity I grasped the problem. They didn't even have to threaten me with exile to the nearest alligator pit!"

"Glib as ever," Eagle retorted, and the arms that held Whitney became stiff and wooden. "What was your previous assignment — a passionate encounter with the Blarney Stone?"

"Mr. Stewart," Whitney said concisely, tossing her head back to meet the icy blue daggers of his eyes with cool emerald, "you are the one who seems to be — ah — full of blarney, shall we say."

"I never lied to you."

Was there a touch of beseechment in his tone? No. That was wishful thinking on her part. His eyes hadn't lost a fraction of their cold hostility; his grip hadn't gentled a shade.

"Omitting the truth is lying," Whitney said miserably. "You made me think you were an Indian — "

The hold that had been stiff was now painful and crushing. "I am an Indian, Miss

Latham. For you to think otherwise — that is deception. I am the man that you met in the swamp that first night — unworthy, uneducated, uncultured — whatever that was to you."

Whitney wanted to protest, to explain that that wasn't what she had meant at all. She couldn't seem to summon breath or form words as he stared down at her, the pride and fury of his forebears stamped rigidly onto a countenance that gave no hint of relenting.

Lowering her eyes with a casual shrug seemed the only way to come to a draw. "What difference does it make? It's obvious that your blond friend doesn't care what you are. Perhaps you should bring me back to my table now and return to her. You've performed your duty on behalf of the councils."

"And you'd like to get back to performing yourself?"

"Pardon?"

"Always such lovely, wide-eyed innocence, Whitney!" Eagle marveled disdainfully. "Your executive over there. I gave you lessons; now you're eager to carry on with practice. He looks like a suitable specimen."

Whitney was dumbstruck. The music, the couples around her, even the man who taunted her blurred together in a seething haze that could only be composed of steam from her own burning body.

How could he possibly think that she could share the absolute intimacy that had raged between them with anyone else? His words sounded like a death knell as they hit her mind with the accuracy of a physical blow. Her nails dug automatically into the palms of her hands and she stiffened with flaming, narrowed eyes, subtly counter-forcing to free herself from his hold with dignity.

But just as subtly his hold switched to the base of her spine and she was dipped back precariously. "Don't try to fight me, Whitney," Eagle warned with mocking men-ace. "You may have come out of your civil little meeting like a water lily, but I wouldn't push on a one-to-one basis."

"You are not a gentleman!" Whitney spat.

"No? Not always, I suppose. But then I seem to remember occasions when your be-havior couldn't quite be called ladylike. Funny — neither of us was offended. In fact, I really didn't mind in the least seeing you be a female instead of a lady — "

Whitney clenched her teeth tightly to-gether and grated, "If there was a civil bone in your body — "

"But there isn't," Eagle interrupted in a

deathly chilling tone. "And not being civil or a gentleman, I tend to say whatever comes into my mind."

Whitney longed to cry that she wanted only to be the female in his arms, but to what end would her words be? His contempt for her was pathetically obvious. He would surely laugh and — worse — return to the lithesome blonde anyway.

Tilting her head back, she smiled at him sweetly through half-closed eyes. "Whatever we are, White Eagle — lady and gentleman or not" — she sniffed disdainfully in opposition to her sultry, feigned grin — "I do suggest we get back to our respective partners. As you say, I'm eager to practice, and it appears that the lady entwined with the bar stool might be hungry to teach the teacher a few new tricks."

There was a combustible moment following her acidic speech when Whitney held her breath in terror, certain that the anger within Eagle would explode and she would be the recipient of unleashed violence. A play of emotions filtered rapidly through his eyes, moving so quickly she couldn't begin to fathom them. His grip, she knew, would leave bruises on her flesh, so tense was it.

Then, miraculously, he released her. "Don't let me hold you up," he said. "Go back to your friend. I don't want to be the cooling factor in anything that might be getting hot. The blonde entwined with the bar stool happens to be my secretary and the tricks she performs are with a typewriter, but you're right, I should get back to her. It would be showing my uncivilized tendencies to leave her any longer."

Eagle nodded briefly and quickly walked away, leaving Whitney on the dance floor, tears brimming in her eyes. Blinking, she made her way through the dancers and out the front door.

Gerry would have to pay the check and follow. She had to get out of the room before she fell apart.

But Eagle wasn't watching her, so he didn't see the unguarded pain that filled her eyes and sent her wretchedly into the night. He was fighting his own lack of control, fiercely battling instincts that demanded he sweep her from the bar and abduct her back to the woods and make love to her over and over until she realized that it could never be the same with anyone else. The idea of her with another man was driving him mad, eating up his insides inch by inch. If he looked at her one more time he would become irrational.

Damnit! He behaved irrationally every

time he saw her now! He, the attorney, the Indian, the man born and trained to ultimate concealment of emotions, allowed himself to be ruled by his possessive anger and to lash out heedlessly when he really meant to crush her in his arms.

The lawyer in his mind told him he had no right.

But the man in him decreed that he did.

And in the space of time it took him to return to the bar and order another drink, the man won the battle.

She was his, although she didn't know it. They had declared their vows before the Supreme Being — One who was surely the same to all men. She was his wife. And he meant to keep her. All the desire, possession, protection, irrationality and anger added up to one thing that made the most complete sense in the world.

He loved her.

CHAPTER NINE

For once in her life Whitney didn't have a single difficulty in dealing with Gerry. She refused point-blank, no nonsense, to answer any of his questions. In unsparing terms she informed him that she was his friend and that was it. He was welcome to be an interested party in her work; he was welcome to view his trip as a visit to a friend.

The rest of her life was none of his business, and, as nicely as possible, he was welcome to tell her father the same thing.

Gerry, as disbelieving as he had been when she asked for the divorce, shook his head with little patience but wisely left her alone at her motel. He wound up having a solitary dinner surrounded by boisterous teenagers at a local hamburger joint.

Whitney spent the night in abject misery. Locked in the privacy of her room, she paced the floor relentlessly, exhausted herself, then threw herself on the bed and moaned for sleep, then paced the floor again. Intermittently she would grow angry, sure she had been used; then the tears would start and she would be sure she had only herself to blame for acting impetuously and speaking without thinking.

Not that it really mattered anymore. Whatever had existed between her and Eagle was now irrevocably over. Maybe she should think up an excuse and run back to Virginia. Here she ran the chance of seeing Eagle again frequently. The tear in her heart would constantly be reopened and she would never have the time needed to heal such a wound.

If time really did heal broken hearts. At the moment she was certain the pain she felt could never be assuaged.

It was close to dawn when exhaustion finally brought her relief in sleep. She felt she had barely closed her eyes when the insistent ringing of the phone brought her back to an unhappy stage of consciousness.

A second of wild hope at the sound of a male voice was immediately dashed.

"It's Gerry," the voice said irritably. "Latham. Remember me? You're still using my name."

"Oh. Good morning. What — ah — time is it?"

"Eight. As a friend, I thought you might be willing to join me for breakfast. In a decent restaurant. I had heartburn all night."

She had to get out of bed, and she had to face the world. She had offered to take him to the new land site, and since she was scheduled for a meeting with the land-fill people and the environmentalists, she should really take a trip for her own benefit. Even if she did decide to tuck tail and request another transfer, she had to keep up with her work until a replacement could be hired, and then she would be required to make damn sure that everything was up to date and handled smoothly.

"Sure, Gerry. The motel has a nice coffee shop. We'll have a good breakfast and I'll show you where the development will be."

"Fifteen minutes?"

"Twenty." Whitney made a face to the phone and hung up.

The face that greeted her in the bathroom mirror looked like hell. Groaning, she showered quickly and spent the remainder of her twenty minutes trying to repair the damage done her by the sleepless night.

Funny how she had felt after a different sleepless night. Then she had been making love, and she had awakened feeling tired but content. The world had been beautiful.

Today she felt as if she should be lowered into the nearest hole in the ground.

"Life goes on," she told her reflection. She had been living without Eagle for weeks now. Why should anything be different?

Because she had thought the land hearings would change everything. Eagle should have raced after her when she left the conference room. He should have told her that he had loved her all along.

She had been living a pipe dream, but real life had intervened. And now she had to face reality. Head on. It wouldn't get any easier. She had lost her heart, but she did still have her pride. And with a good base coat of makeup over the shadows beneath her eyes, no one else would ever need to know that the dream in her life was over.

A light touch of blush took the white hue from her face. What the heck, she told herself, applying a light green shadow and brown mascara. Go all the way. With a coat of moist lipstick, she actually looked good.

Or so she thought.

"You look like hell," Gerry told her.

"So I've been told," she replied, adding silently, by myself! "Could we forget me and my looks for a while?" she begged. "Tell me about home. How is my mom doing with her garden?"

Gerry amicably kept the conversation light while they ate, filling her in on all the little happenings since she had left Richmond. His tone remained easy the entire morning, until Whitney drove to Alligator Alley and down the path that led to the proposed sight in a company jeep.

Reaching the land filled Whitney with a sense of contentment and keen satisfaction. It was largely marsh right now, but she had been assured that filling the area was highly feasible without causing damage to the expanse of the Everglades. She could envision the planned community — affordable, pleasant, widely spaced homes that were encircled by the natural beauty of the area. Children would live in the homes, and they would have old-fashioned swings tied to the sturdy branches of the old cypress trees. The builders would work around the canals and lakes, and the unusual animal life would not be uprooted from its natural habitat.

Gerry was not sharing her future vision, Whitney realized quickly. He began ranting as his shoe slipped in the mud while he followed her on a short footpath that led to a 'gator hole.

"This is it, Whitney! The grand finale!

That you haven't already killed yourself is amazing! Why on earth do you want to wander around this horrible hellhole anyway? Damnation!" He swatted viciously at a mosquito. "Dratted things. What the hell else is around here? Snakes, I'm sure. And God only knows what other creatures. You're going to need a fumigation squad before anything else! And it isn't for you. I never saw you swat a fly, Whitney. You look nice in dresses, not mud. We are going to leave this minute, and if you won't listen to me I'll have your father down here — "

"Gerry!" Whitney shouted his name in disgust. "My father cannot send me to my room! Neither can you! I live here now. And I'll be spending many days in this 'hellhole.' Christ, Gerry, look around you with an open mind! There's beauty here, Gerry. If you can't see it, I do! And I'm not budging. You go back to Virginia! Tell my father whatever you want. And if he can't appreciate any of this, he can just go home, too!"

"Whitney!" Gerry gasped. "What has gotten into you? Have you no respect for the man who raised you? I just can't believe this. I refuse to believe this!" He set a slim hand over hers with purpose. "We are leaving now. You don't know what you're doing, and somebody has to take responsibility for you."

"I am not going anywhere! I have things to see here. When I finish I will take you back to the city. And then I'll drive you to the airport!"

Gerry's hand didn't move. He stared at Whitney as if she were a belligerent child.

"Excuse me, but I think you heard the lady. Let her go."

Both Whitney and Gerry spun in the direction of the softly spoken but forceful, determined words. Neither had heard a thing in the wilderness to warn them that a third party had come upon them.

A weakness came into Whitney's system. It was Eagle.

He was all Miccosukee as he stood before them, his legs apart in tight jeans, his arms crossed over a chest that was covered by a braided jacket. His blue-raven hair gleamed in the traces of light that shimmered around him.

The look in his brilliant eyes was all challenge, all warrior.

"Who the hell are you?" Gerry demanded.

Eagle raised a single, imperious brow and advanced toward them with his cat tread. "What difference does that make?"

Whitney had to stifle a smile. Poor Gerry! He was in beyond his league, and he didn't recognize the man from the previous evening.

How could her ex be so blind, Whitney wondered. She would recognize Eagle's piercing blue eyes and majestic stance if he were dyed green and covered in snow!

"It makes a tremendous difference!" Gerry said heatedly, confused but refusing to be daunted by an Indian in the woods. "You're interrupting a private matter between a husband and wife — "

"She is no longer your wife," Eagle interrupted quietly.

"What?" Gerry stuttered.

"She is no longer your wife."

"All right, then! Ex-wife! But I'm responsible for her well-being and she doesn't know what she's doing out here and I'm taking her back to the civilized world!"

"Whitney is free and over twenty-one. Where she chooses to be is her own concern."

"Whitney!" Gerry repeated explosively. He stared at her accusingly. "You know this man?"

"Yes. I do," Whitney said quickly. She felt as if she had been watching a tennis match, following the ball back and forth across the net, an observer, not a participant.

"All right, so you know my wife — " Gerry began again to Eagle.

"Ex-wife. I underline 'ex,'" Eagle said calmly.

"Ex. Ex, ex," Gerry sputtered. "What difference does it make to you? This is a private matter and none of your business."

"This is very much my business," Eagle replied with deadly certainty. "I find Whitney to be rather capable. I believe she knows exactly what she is doing out here. It is her right to stay. As to my rights — well" — he allowed his gaze to roam contemplatively over Whitney, the slightest hint of a mischievous twinkle in the depths of his blue eyes — "that, sir, is why I find myself stressing the preface 'ex.' You see, the lady is my wife now. And although I find her completely responsible myself, I assure you that you have no need to worry yourself over her further. I take that upon myself."

Whitney didn't know whether to cry or to burst into laughter. Gerry's amazed statement voiced her sentiments exactly.

"I don't believe this!" he ejaculated.

What was going on, Whitney wondered. Did Eagle mean what he was saying? Did he really consider her his wife? More likely he had stumbled upon them and simply decided to help her — now that he knew who Gerry was — out of simple pity. Perhaps he felt he owed her one because of the land.

"Believe what you like, Mr. Latham," Eagle said with a shrug. "But Whitney and I were married almost a month ago. Just a few days after she came south. It was one of those shotgun affairs" — Whitney could clearly see the teasing light beneath the darkly arched brows — "except it was my grandmother after us instead of the usual bride's father."

"This is preposterous!" Gerry stated rigidly. "Whitney, is this true?"

"Yes — "

"It can't be legal! You're not tied to this — this — "

"Indian?" Whitney supplied innocently.

Gerry glanced at her reproachfully. "This man," he said indignantly. His eyes narrowed as he looked at Eagle, then widened as dawning comprehension came into them. "The restaurant!" he exclaimed. "That was you — "

"Yes," Eagle said pleasantly. "That was me. And while we're on the subject, my name is Stewart. Legally, that is. And you do seem to be concerned with legalities."

"I'm a lawyer — " Gerry began.

"So am I," Eagle interrupted, waving a hand coolly in dismissal, "and as such, sir, I've learned that human nature has little to do with the law. It's my understanding that you and Whitney have no legal ties. And yet you are here, and she is with you. That is a tie, one that goes beyond a piece of paper. I believe that you are legitimately concerned for her, and that she cares for you — as a friend. That's why I'm making such an effort to maintain patience." He walked forward to them on his silent tread until he stood just a foot away from Whitney, and though he continued to speak as if he were addressing Gerry, his eyes were hypnotically locked on hers. "However legal that ceremony was, Whitney is tied to me. I think she knows it." For a moment he continued to stare at her, and the hammock in the woods was held in an eerie silence, as if time had stopped and they all waited in suspended animation. Whitney was suddenly keenly aware of all the little sounds in the cypress glen: the breeze rustling softly through moss and sawgrass, the drone of a fly, the light crackle of dipping branches.

And she was aware of Eagle. He did not touch her, yet he did. It seemed as if the blue steel of his eyes bore through her, searching out her soul, commanding her heart. But she didn't dare move or speak; his eyes were as hard and relentless as his ramrod stance, and fathomless. Was he telling her that they were even, that the score had been settled?

Or was he really staking a claim to her?

He stepped back and turned once more to Gerry. "I hope," he said with a slight edge of contempt, "that I shall never need to depend on a legality or a piece of paper to hold what is mine. Should that ever be the case, I doubt if there would really be anything to keep." He nodded grimly to Gerry, pivoted and started back up the path.

Immobilized, Whitney watched him until his broad shoulders disappeared into the brush. Then her feet took flight, and completely forgetting Gerry, she raced after him, to catch him breathlessly as he was hopping into his own jeep, which was parked behind hers.

"Eagle!" She shouted his name, but as he settled into the driver's seat and acknowledged her, her throat constricted and her words refused to come. There wasn't a hint of softening in the blue chill of his eyes, nor did he encourage her to come to him in any way. Halting a few steps from the jeep, she stared at him blankly, at a loss.

"Yes?"

"Thank you," she said inanely.

Did she imagine it? Or did a trace of disappointment filter through the glacial blue steel?

"Not at all," he said wryly. "Is that it?"

"I — I — " she floundered.

Muttering an impatient oath, Eagle sprang from the jeep. Stalking her roughly, he gripped her shoulders with tense fingers that bit into her flesh. She winced, but he didn't care. He had come to claim her, simply to demand her by right. And if he stayed much longer, he would.

But the scene he had come upon had changed his mind. At first he had wanted to act like any normal jealous male and rip Whitney away from the man who threatened her, shove her protectively behind his back and simply proceed to settle the matter with his fists.

But something had held him back. It might have even been pity. Gerry Latham was not really his rival. It was clear that he no longer had any hold on Whitney. Despite his highhanded tactics, it was pathetically obvious that he still loved his ex-wife.

Without thinking, or rather because he had been thinking, Eagle gave Whitney a rough shake. And where she was tongue-tied, he found words he never meant to say tumbling curtly from his mouth.

"What is he doing here? Why have you brought him out here to begin with?"

Whitney slowly leaned her head back so that her hair fell behind her in a long, dark wave and her emerald eyes met his. They had been strangely blank; now they turned tremulous, and then defiant, and Eagle wished fervently that he had handled the whole matter differently.

He had meant what he said to Gerry — Whitney was his, but only because the tie would be of her own choosing.

And that was the way he wanted it.

"Do I owe you an explanation?" Whitney demanded.

"Yes," Eagle said, and softly added, "if you feel that you do."

Before she could answer him, Eagle pulled her to him and his lips descended over hers. They came down hard, and the punishing grip on her shoulders shifted to the small of her back, pressing her to him.

Her form was pliant. It molded to his, which was what he wanted. He wanted her to feel his strength and heat, the way his hands could take her delicate form, the way his body could press to her with natural need.

Then, as she clung to him with the response he had barely dared hope for, had desired with all his heart, his kiss took on a subtle change, teasing softly, his tongue parrying lightly where it had plundered.

He was gambling.

She was arched to him, straining against him; the fullness of her soft breasts crushed into his chest, begging to be held and caressed.

Eagle allowed his hands to move enticingly along her back. His fingers roamed just beneath the material of her shirt, inch by inch up her ribs. . . .

And then he pulled away.

Whitney was stunned. She blinked, and then a flood of humiliation washed through her at the ease with which he could draw complete capitulation from her and then coolly set her aside. What was it the man really wanted? Shakily she opened her mouth to say something — anything — as long as it was suitably scathing,

"I — " was as far as she got.

"You," Eagle interrupted, and as his crystal gaze held her he was a cross between that man who had boldly declared himself to Gerry in no uncertain terms with assured control and the one who had leaped from the jeep to claim her, "have some thinking to do. And" — he lifted a brow and tilted his head toward the path where they could now hear Gerry stumbling through the brush — "a little unfinished business to attend to." Running a finger lightly from the tip of a high cheekbone to her chin, he added huskily, "You have to decide just where your ties are, Whitney. I want you, but though I don't wish to subjugate you, I promise that being mine, I will be the dominating force in your life. As you will be — and have been — in my own." His lips curled ruefully at the corners. "I'm learning that I can be very dominating, demanding and possessive where you're concerned. But you hold the cards, my love. The final play is yours. I've told you what is, what will be. The choice is yours." He tapped the tip of her nose lightly. "If you want me, Whitney, come to me."

The trees near the clearing were beginning to crackle as Gerry, muttering curses to the mosquitoes and the uneven path, neared them. Eagle smiled briefly and both brows raised in sardonic amusement. "Pick a husband, Whitney. Personally, it's my suggestion that you get that one back on a plane for Richmond. He may not be a bad guy — it's obvious that he does care about you — but he's dismally out of place here. And with you — I know that now. I guess I knew it from the beginning; I just needed to *feel* it."

With a last little salute he spun around and vaulted back into the jeep. Whitney, still searching for her tongue, stared after him, amazed. She had listened with virtual speechlessness to all he had had to say, and after his first angry questions, he hadn't expected a single answer. He had told her to come to him, and then he had walked away.

"Whitney!" Gerry stumbled from the trees, dusting his cuffs, as Eagle's jeep graveled away in a cloud of dust.

"You didn't have to leave me alone!" Gerry grumbled gruffly. Whitney finally peeled her eyes from the disappearing vehicle to turn distractedly to her ex-husband. "What?"

"Oh, never mind." Oddly enough, Gerry seemed amused. He set an arm lightly around her shoulders. "Get me out of here, will you? Then you can get back to your Indian."

"Pardon?"

"Listen, Whitney," Gerry said with a smile, still brushing at his clothing uneasily, "on that score I don't need a road map." He flicked a tendril of her hair softly from her face with a sigh of sadness. "Whitney, I did come here for the wrong reasons. I wanted to bring you back to Richmond — and back to me. But Stewart had some things to say that made sense. And more than that, Whit, I saw the way you looked at him. You never looked at me like that."

"Oh, Gerry," Whitney said miserably.

"Don't," Gerry interrupted, "it's okay." He headed for the jeep. "Shall I drive?"

Whitney nodded mutely and climbed in beside him. Her heart, mind and emotions

261

were spinning crazy cartwheels.

Eagle had come to the Glades to find her. In straight terms he had announced that he believed in her, he had defended her in front of Gerry. . . .

And he had claimed her as his — if that was what she wanted.

Even his brief streak of jealousy had come quickly under control. He was a towering pinnacle of strength, one that neither suffocated nor strangled but stood sturdy, offering support.

She had really been a fool, allowing anger and pride to come between them. She had walked out on him once without giving him a chance at explanation.

And since then she had given him little but argument.

Now she had a chance to walk back into his life. Many things still needed to be said on both sides, but they were all so inconsequential.

A small smile curved her lips. He had threatened to dominate, but she was learning that love's domination could be a wonderful thing. It did not hinder or bind but led to growth and wove those webs that were of one's own choosing.

All she needed now was nerve. And belief.

Cartwheels were churning in her stomach

again. It would be so hard to go to him! Already niggling doubts were worming their way into her resolution.

Had he really said he wanted her? And, she wondered wistfully, did he love her?

He had yet to say the words.

CHAPTER TEN

True to his word, Gerry was ready to take the first available shuttle out of Naples. In less than two hours since they left the Glades, Whitney was standing with him before the gate that led to his small plane.

With his hands upon her shoulders, he smiled affectionately and kissed both her cheeks. "Good luck, Whitney."

Impulsively Whitney hugged him back. "The right woman is out there for you somewhere, Gerry, and when you find her you'll know it beyond a doubt."

"Oh? How?" he asked skeptically.

"Skyrockets!" she told him impishly. "You'd better get on that plane."

And then she watched as her "unfinished business" rumbled, circled and flew north.

It was showdown time, and her nerves began to jitter even as she left the airport. And as she had once wondered in the waters of the hammock lake, her question was, Where is that damned man?

Come to me. Where? And then she was suddenly sure. He had gone to the place where they had sealed the vows of their love before any commitment had been spoken.

Nervous but determined to follow her course, Whitney stopped at her room and called her office to announce that she would be gone for a few days. Susie cheerfully accepted her message and then had one to give her.

"Mr. Stewart called for you this morning. I told him I believed you had gone to the land site. Did he ever get hold of you?"

"Yes," Whitney said and smiled. "He certainly did."

Saying good-bye, she slowly replaced the receiver, elation adding to her jitters.

Eagle had not just stumbled upon her. He had come out purposely to find her.

Slow, she told her pounding heart. Before she allowed herself to take flight in dreams, she still had much to do, and she had to be sure. . . .

Picking up the phone again, she dialed his office. She could now picture the soft-spoken blonde who informed her that Eagle Stewart had left the office early that morning and would be out indefinitely on personal business.

This time her hand was shaking so badly she had to fumble with the receiver twice before she reset it correctly. She was holding a very special happiness in the palm of her hand.

Don't let me lose it, God! she prayed silently.

There was one more call she had to make — the hardest. But the day was fading fast, and there was only one way she knew of to reach the Eagle settlement deep in the Glades. . . .

Flipping through her address book, she found the number for the Big Cypress Reservation. As she was passed from person to person and put on hold, desperation began to grow within her, a stifled sob catching in her throat as she waited.

She had to reach Eagle today. She couldn't bear another night of uncertainty . . . and if she waited, the doubts and fears would come back full force and she might lose her chance.

"Randy!" She breathed a sigh of relief as he finally came to the phone. "I really hate to do this to you again," she began after he had happily greeted her. "But I need another favor. This time I have to get back *into* the reservation. I have to find Eagle, and I'm sure he must be out with Morning Dew. Randy, I know you must be busy, but is there any way you could get me out there today?"

Randy chuckled, and Whitney could well imagine him grinning on the other end of the wire. He would be wearing that lopsided smile that stated he found women irrational yet wonderful little creatures that needed to be humored. Maybe he was feeling like a smug-as-pie matchmaker.

Whitney didn't care. As long as he felt like humoring her at the moment.

"I'm sure I can work something out, Whitney. Go on out to Eagle's cabin in the woods, and I'll round up Katie and meet you as soon as possible. You do know the way to the cabin?"

"By heart," Whitney replied wryly.

"Good. Then see you soon."

Whitney was standing and grabbing her shoulder bag before they could say good-bye. She raced out of her room and to the BMW and out once more to Alligator Alley.

A rueful smile curved her lips as she pulled into the long dirt drive that led to the cabin. Had it only been a month since she had first followed this trail — a different

Whitney, so sure of her convictions?

It had all started here, a slow process of learning, taught by a man of quiet strength whom she had given herself to before she had begun to understand. It was almost as if fate had sent her, frightened and blind, down this trail and directly into the arms of the man who would open her eyes to love.

Randy arrived with Katie in just moments, and they set out together in the jeep. Neither of the Harrises had any questions or comments to make about her mad desire to see Eagle as soon as possible; indeed, they acted as if her calling them to rush from work to take the long ride into the heart of the swamp was the most natural thing in the world.

Their conversation was casual yet strangely close and intimate in the jeep. Once they had begun the trek through the sawgrass in the airboat, they all had little to say.

Whitney scanned the acres of marshland with growing trepidation. Was this what Eagle had meant? Was her coming to him in the deep Glades the sign of trust he needed?

"Pa hay okee," Katie said softly.

"Pardon?" Whitney was jolted from her fearful reflections to turn to her.

"Pa hay okee," Katie repeated, spreading her arms to encompass the land they streaked through. "River of grass. It is our homeland; it succors and supports us, because we love and cherish it for all that it is. I think it is your homeland, too, Whitney."

"Pa hay okee," Whitney whispered, smiling at Katie. She didn't need to say any more; a slender bond existed between the two women, one of the ties Eagle had spoken of, born of friendship, understanding and mutual respect.

When Randy finally pulled off to the high hammock of the Eagle clan, Whitney felt her nervous jitters escalate into full-scale, trembling fear. The closer she came to that which she most desired, the more terrified she became of rejection. Reason warred against her fears. All those things Eagle had said! The way he had held her . . . the way he had kissed her. He had to really want her! Still, she was grateful for the company of Katie and Randy.

Except, she discovered, she was about to lose that company.

Katie kissed her cheek. "See you later, Whitney. I'm going to like having a sister!"

Were these people all mind readers, Whitney wondered as she quickly demanded, "Where are you going? Aren't you going to stop and see your grandmother? Randy? I'm sure Morning Dew will be very upset if you don't — "

"I think," Randy interrupted gently, "that Morning Dew is probably expecting you. My brother-in-law may be sweating it out a bit, but Morning Dew isn't. You go on, Whitney. This is your family, too. This is your special time. Find Eagle."

Whitney's eyes darted from Harris to Harris. It was a little late for doubt, but she was riddled with it. Was Eagle really here, waiting?

"Katie — "

"Whitney, go on!" Katie laughed as the airboat propeller began to spin. The craft moved off into the marsh and Katie waved and called, "You will find him!"

Alone, Whitney fought the butterflies in her stomach and searched out the little trail in the cypress. A moment later she came upon the village. The women and children acknowledged her with smiles and words of greeting.

They were not surprised to see her.

Following the second trail, Whitney came to Morning Dew. The old woman with the keen, bright eyes and weathered face was sitting before the cooking fire, complacently sewing. She didn't look up until Whitney stood before her; then she smiled as if welcoming a child who had made it home promptly on time for dinner. Whitney knelt beside her and took a gnarled and workworn hand into her own.

How much did Morning Dew know, Whitney wondered. What did she think of her disappearance from the Corn Dance? Would she understand how long the road had been?

The Indian woman stared at her with gentle eyes that seemed omniscient and all understanding. Whitney realized she needed no explanations; there would be nothing new that she could tell her.

"Eagle," she whispered simply, controlling the tone of desperation that was edging her voice. "Eagle," she practically sobbed. "Oh, Morning Dew! Do you know where he is?"

"Hush, little one," Morning Dew soothed in her perfect, unaccented English. "He is here. Where your heart has led you. He is by the lake. He waits." Her wizened features formed a grimace. "Eagle is not all Indian, you know, and right now he is living with a white man's fears. You must go to him and calm his soul and your own. He has not put his faith in the laws of the spirits."

Whitney bit her lip lightly, afraid to leave the absolute conviction of the older woman.

"Go now," Morning Dew prodded. "We will have time, you and I, later. Years to learn better of one another. But now you must go. My grandson — your husband — awaits you."

Whitney needed no further urging. With a last smile for Morning Dew, she raced down the trail to the lake with her heart plummeting crazily. She sped through the cypress as if chased by the devil, then halted, mesmerized by shivering apprehension.

Here she was, in the swamp, by the lake, where her journey had taken her. But what now? Oh God, what now? What did she say?

And Eagle was there. She saw his back first, rippled with tight muscles and bared to glow bronze beneath the dying sun. She itched to run her fingers over the sleek skin of his broad shoulders and press her lips against his flesh, to reach up and touch the thick raven hair. . . .

But she held back. He hadn't seen her yet. She couldn't see his eyes, couldn't read into his heart.

He turned suddenly, knowing that she was there, framed by the ridge of the cypress. Whitney's breath caught in her throat. He was just staring at her, his hands in the pockets of his form-hugging jeans. A gentle lash of waves from the quiet lake washed over his feet, soaking his pants legs, but he didn't seem to notice. He was frozen like a statue, watching her, his blue gaze startling and compelling but fathomless.

The man who stood as solidly as an oak was trembling inside like a young boy. She had come! Guided by the chemistry of hearts and minds that beat together, she had sought him out. As he watched her, her quivering immobility between the flanking cypress trees, he thought lovingly of all that she was. So delicate beside him! Yet like the beautiful orchids of the Everglades, she was strong and tenacious. From that very first night he had loved her, although he had fought against it. And now he wanted to speak; he wanted to reach out and touch the petal softness of her face. He needed to take her into his arms and promise that they would never be apart again.

Whitney was growing desperate. Damn him! She had come all this way, and he wasn't saying a thing! If his relentless stare of steel persisted much longer, she would run screaming back into the woods.

No, she had come this far. If it was another step that she must take first, then she must take that step.

What could she say? How could she begin?

Maybe it was one of those times when action would say more than words. And time to turn the tables a little.

She was shaking, but a show of bravado could be perpetuated. Leaving the haven of the trees, Whitney stalked slowly toward the lake, keeping her eyes locked with Eagle's. He followed her every movement but still stood silent.

Three feet from the water Whitney began to undo the buttons of her blouse. Removing the garment with a sultry lack of haste, she tossed it to him, smiling mischievously when his reflexes forced him to catch it. With slow deliberation she stooped, unzipped her boots and kicked them nonchalantly aside.

It was the first strip-tease she had ever performed, and it was hard to calculate its effect on her audience, but feminine instinct told her it was going well. Eagle hadn't spoken, but the pulses in his neck were becoming fast and erratic. A feeling of happy power was coming over her. The desire she was hoping to elicit made sultry emeralds of her eyes, and she shimmied from her jeans with a tantalizing rhythm.

Eagle could have moved then. He could have reached out, crushed her to him and allowed his hard, burning body to demand all that she was offering. But he waited, now with tender, aching amusement. What she was doing was sheer torture, yet it was the sweetest bliss! His body was as taut as a thinly stretched tightrope; his nerves clamored in a cry of thrill and agony for him simply to force her curvaceous, taunting form into his arms and take her with blunt command to appease the rising passion that strained to be released.

But somehow he knew it would be worth it to wait, as he had already waited all these weeks. The smile that was slowly curving his lips was an assured one; he would soon reap his just rewards for superhuman patience.

Whitney saw the smile and her heart skipped a beat. What she had begun, she knew beyond a shadow of a doubt, he would finish. Her fingers suddenly became leaden, and as she slipped the stubborn hooks of her French-cut bra and hastily discarded her panties, her cool was somewhat lost. Not all that practiced at being a seductress, her nerve was ebbing, especially as she realized that the eyes watching her had gone a murky midnight blue that promised of things to come. . . .

Whitney ran her fingers through her dark hair and tossed her head back. Feigning complete innocence, she plunged into the deliciously cool water, swam a bit for distance and rose like a mermaid from the depths. Water streamed from her hair and over her breasts in tiny rivulets of crystal. Watching from the shore, Eagle shuddered as a jolt of flaming, uncontrollable desire burst inside him and ripped its way through his entire length.

"Join me?" she teased breathlessly. "I assure you, I will not attack you." Her voice lowered a shade and the husky tone held a note of beseechment. "It is your move, White Eagle."

It was his move all right, Eagle groaned to himself, but could he make it to the water? He'd never had more trouble unbuckling a belt in his life.

"Hey, there!" Whitney laughed. "What's the problem, Flapping Feather? Get in here!"

Eagle grinned. He finally managed to undo the brass buckle and release the fly on his pants. "What's the hurry?" he drawled. "I mean, after all, honey, if you *don't* attack. . . ."

His voice trailed away as his clothes fell to

the dust and he entered the water in all his natural, ultravirile, male splendor.

"Even the best of us can be provoked," Whitney murmured.

His raven head suddenly disappeared beneath the water, and Whitney caught her breath. She plunged below the surface herself and began to swim blindly in an elusive manner. It was a foolish gesture. She would never outmatch his prowess in the water.

A powerful hand clamped around her ankle and she sputtered awkwardly to the top, flailing for balance as he continued to hold her foot high.

"Let go of my foot!" Whitney demanded in between a fit of giggles. "You uncouth rogue!"

"As you say, madame," Eagle replied politely. He jerked her foot and released it, sending her back to the bottom.

Whitney rose to the surface gasping. "Okay, Flapping Feather!" she choked. "This is it. You will get yours!"

Eagle's blue eyes danced with a hellfire. "Oh, I do hope so!" he declared. "I'm counting on it."

Whitney crashed through the water and into his arms. Her breasts crushed into his chest and the nipples hardened at the sizzling contact. Her face nestled into the curve of his neck and she clung to him, radiating in the simple ecstasy of being back where she belonged, of feeling their hearts beat as one.

Eagle caught the hair at the base of her neck and forced her to face him. The bronze skin was stretched tautly over his proud features; the dancing light in his eyes had been replaced by the smoldering cobalt blue. "Are you sure you don't want to talk first, Whitney?" he demanded harshly.

"No!" She shook her head vehemently.

He held her tensely for a second and then sighed his relief. "Good. I don't think I could do much talking."

His lips came down on hers with a fierce possessiveness that left her quaking and gasping for more. Then his head disappeared beneath the water again, but this time his game was in earnest. His teeth moved over a nipple with a gentle tug that sent sparks igniting to her core. Then his erotic water kisses and nibbles moved leisurely all the way down to her toes. When he surfaced again, it was to scoop her into his arms.

Whitney's breath was coming in short pants as she slipped her arms around his neck and looked tenderly into his beloved face. "Much more of that and I could quite cheerfully drown," she purred huskily in spurts of air. "I'm glad we're heading for shore."

"We may not make shore," he muttered hoarsely. His arms tightened around her and his murky-lashed lids fell so that his eyes were sensuous slits. "And I intend that you should drown, my love. Drown in me forever."

They reached the shore — just. Eagle set her down gently so that the water still washed in ripples along her legs.

Then he moved over her, and foreplay was discarded as they both emitted strangled groans and became entwined in a desperate and urgent mutual hunger. Tears of unprecedented joy came to Whitney's eyes as their unleashed passion raged to new pinnacles of erotic, shattering, mystical sensation and Eagle urged her ever onward, telling her of his gnawing need, of the awesome pleasure of all that she did, of the perfection and beauty of her undulating hips.

The culmination of their fierce intensity was explosive. Whitney's cry of sweet, sweet ecstasy rent the twilight air, and before its echo had settled into the sheltering cypress, she was moaning slightly, her contentment so great that the world continued to swirl until her form slowly, slowly began to relax.

As always, Eagle held her tightly to him as they regained their footing on solid earth, his touch gentle and soothing now, no longer a rough and demanding magic.

He was glorious when he made love, Whitney decided. Most delightfully glorious. She wouldn't have it any other way.

He shifted after a moment and leaned on an elbow to watch her as he ran enticing patterns over her belly.

"I love you, you know," he said with velvet softness. "More than I'll ever be able to tell you. I'm not sure exactly how or when, but you wound me hopelessly around that delicate little finger of yours."

Whitney inched more closely to his chest, relishing the wonderful masculine scent of him. "I love you."

"I want to marry you in a church as soon as possible."

Whitney chuckled. "That's lovely, darling, and I'd like it very much. But, my dear Jonathan White Eagle Stewart, you had better start considering yourself a married man right now. You have had a wife since the first night of the Corn Dance."

"Oh? Is that so?" Moving with his startling agility, he pounced over her and his eyes blazed with teasing menace into hers. "Then you'd better consider this! Don't you dare — ever! — get it into your mind to pull another disappearing act or I'll skin you alive and tan your hide! Got it?"

"Yes, sir, yes, sir!" Whitney pledged with mock, round-eyed obedience. "But, Counselor, I only plead guilty with an explanation to the first charge! You were leading me down a primrose trail and laughing your rear off all the while."

"No, I wasn't, Whitney," Eagle said, suddenly serious. "I admit I did want to get to you, but it was more than that. I knew there was something special about you from the moment I plucked you from the mud. Even when you were being an impudent snob, I really wanted you to understand. It was important to me that you realize chickees were not hovels, and, of course, that I do speak English. Rather well, in fact."

"Oh, quit!" Whitney pleaded. "Won't you ever let me live that down."

"Never, love. I cherish all my memories too dearly."

Whitney frowned suddenly and ran her fingers tenderly down his cheek. "So do I," she whispered. "Especially my memory of this morning. But I don't understand. After last night — "

"Last night," Eagle said sheepishly, running his fingers through her hair, "I behaved like a thwarted lover. I had no idea whom you were with, and seeing you with another man — when I had become sure we could work things out — drove me half wild. Then I began to cool down, realizing things weren't always what they seemed. You had thought I was 'with' my secretary. I finally put two and two together. I realized the man you were with had to be the infamous Gerry. I had ribbed you cruelly because of simple jealousy. And as far as I was concerned, too, darling, you were already my wife. It frustrated the hell out of me not to be able to do anything about it! I called your office in the morning, determined to have an honest showdown, and they told me you were going out to the land site. I decided to follow you."

"Thank God you did!"

Eagle's brows knit tightly together. "At first I wanted to strangle that ex-husband of yours. I knew a lot about your relationship, but he was with you, and love isn't always rational. He didn't look like a terrible person. Are you sure it's over?"

"I never said Gerry was a terrible person!" Whitney laughed. "He was amazingly decent after your appearance. He was as positive as I that it was all over. He told me to go to you, and I put him on a plane. Everything is over for me that doesn't concern a wonderfully crazy Indian attorney!"

Whitney's eyes shone with bright emerald love, and their track of conversation was temporarily lost as Eagle kissed her with gentle sweetness, savoring the magic moments of revelation. When he finally pulled away, it was to draw a long, shaky breath. "Where were we?" he murmured, bewildered at the way he could lose himself completely in her enchanting warmth.

"Right here, love," Whitney whispered dreamily.

"Now wait a minute, wanton witch," Eagle said with a laugh, catching the slender hand that teased along the length of his back. "I have a few questions. What made you change your mind when it was so stubbornly set? About the land, and me."

"It was simple — your father told me I was trying to build on a burial ground. Then your sister convinced me that you were right — culture and custom mean more to many people than convenience and electric stoves. I'm really a very reasonable person!"

"Hah!"

"I am."

"It may take you a few years to convince me of that," Eagle said with a chuckle, running a finger over her lips with thorough fascination. "So that old coot of a father of mine went after you, huh? No wonder he was so smug about things working out!"

"He's something special," Whitney said softly. "And I'm very grateful to him! Without him, there wouldn't be a you!" She raised a questioning brow. "Is he still in town? He told me he lived in Chicago."

"Yeah, he's still in town. He told me he missed the first wedding so he wanted to hang around for the second!"

Whitney giggled. "I think you're all a pack of Hindu mystics, not Indians! By the way," she demanded, "just what will my name be?"

"Mrs. Jonathan Eagle Stewart, of course."

"Of course!" she mimicked with an impish grin. "And where will we really live?"

"We" — Eagle scowled — "will really live at my permanent address — a nice little house in a pretty beach section of Naples called Port Royal. However, I do own the cabin in the woods. And I have permanent reservations for a certain chickee. Do you mind?"

"Not in the least," Whitney assured him innocently. "Although I admit I'm not certain I could spend my life in a chickee, I have become partial to certain of the dwellings. And I love rustic little cabins in the woods. Besides, my love," she told him huskily, "my ties are firmly knotted. I would sleep with you anywhere."

"Sleeping wasn't exactly what I had in mind," Eagle declared with silky insinuation. "Not yet, anyway. Strenuous activity before bedtime is known to improve the quality of your rest. Did you know that?"

"No. Really?" Whitney fluttered her lashes guilelessly and ran a taunting finger lightly over his taut abdomen, delighting in the quiver and sharp intake of breath that were his response. "Then, since we seem to be busy people who need their rest, I suggest we engage in lots of strenuous activity."

Eagle laughed and pulled her tightly to his hardening body. "A most pleasurable suggestion." His lips began a knowing forage against the sensitive flesh of her throat.

"Ummmmm . . ." Whitney murmured, allowing her fingers the wonder of sinking possessively into his sleek raven hair.

He continued to play upon her body with expertise and draw from it the response of a beautiful, perfectly tuned instrument.

The golden globe of a shimmering orange sun sank slowly in its descent into the horizon. The light was dazzling upon the glassy water in reflection and cast graceful shadows upon the birds caught in silhouette like shadows in the dusk. For a second Whitney mused upon the vivid, primitive loveliness of the land she could now call home.

Then it all became part of a splendor that was rightfully hers. Her lover claimed her undivided attention again and she was among those that soared the gold-streaked skies, in flight with an eagle forever.